Mail-Order Gambler

Sarah Lamb

A thank you to my proofreader, Brooke, and all of the lovely women who help ARC read to catch those typos I miss!

This book was not written by AI. Any typos are proudly (and embarrassingly!) my own human created ones!

ISBN: Paperback ISBN: 978-1-960418-33-3
ISBN Large Print: ISBN: 978-1-960418-34-0

Contents

To all those who take a chance every day on finding happiness, even when the gamble may not pay off. One day, it will.

Chapter 1

1877 Hackberry Falls, Kansas

The sun beat down on Kody Hall. It was hot out, even with his wide-brimmed hat providing a little bit of shade. A dog bolted across the dusty street, with two children close by and shrieking as they chased after it.

He continued walking, but watched with a smile as the dog stopped, shook its tail, gave a little yip, and then set off again. Must have been a game they were playing. So far, everyone he'd passed today had been smiling. Seemed the perfect day for it. Blue skies, sunshine, and wide-open spaces.

Just what a man, woman, or child needed after the harsh winter they'd come through. Kody himself was enjoying being outside every second he could.

He continued down the street, and the sounds of laughter drifted from a nearby building. Kody instinctively turned his head toward it and just as quickly wished he hadn't.

The saloon rose in front of him and he paused. No, that wasn't the truth. His legs locked up, his feet planting themselves right before the building. Kody swallowed hard. Tried to ignore that little itch in him that suggested he stop inside. Get a drink. Play a hand or two at cards.

A couple of ranch hands walked past, and one glanced at him. "Coming in?" he asked, holding the swinging door open.

"Not today." Kody grinned, even as his toes wanted to tap to the song playing within. He'd always had a soft spot for that one. "I gave all that up. Trying to go respectable."

The hand laughed. "That so?"

"That's so." Kody winked.

"Must be a woman," Carl, the local old-timer, hooted from one of the chairs out front. "Can't be nothin' else."

Kody laughed, but didn't answer. What could he say? Carl was right. He'd been trading letters with a woman for a few months now. It might go somewhere, it might not, but fact of the matter was she—like every respectable woman—wouldn't have approved of him being in a saloon, nor the fact he was a gambler at heart.

Waving goodbye with a two-finger salute, Kody wandered toward the spring a ways off. There was always fresh, cool, clear water to slake a man's thirst. Today would be no different.

He reached the spring. When the spring had first been discovered bubbling up from the large rock, some men had chipped away at the stone a little more to make a basin, where one could more easily fill a cup or a bucket. The tinsmith had crafted a large mug, and had tied it to a stake, so anyone passing by could relieve their thirst.

Kody was grateful for that, as he filled the mug and drank deeply, the cold water a shock to his hot body. It felt refreshing. Eased his thirst. But it didn't do anything for that itch. Kody's eyes narrowed, and he took some slow breaths. He wasn't going in. Not going back.

Fact of the matter, though, was it was hard. Real hard.

Gambling was something Kody had been doing near since birth. It wasn't because he was addicted to a win. No, he was *good* at it. From the early days of betting on whose frog would cross a line first, or whose marble would roll furthest to betting on who would go out with Sara Lee Jenkins, all the way to cards, business deals and... Well, anyone who knew him would get the point.

There wasn't a thing he wouldn't bet on. Usually.

Kody just had a sense about it all. He knew how to pick the best frog. How much effort to put forth on a marble. Just what those creases in the corner of a man's eyes or the tension in his jaw meant.

Gambling was a *skill*. And every man ought to have one.

And every man should know when he should stop. For Kody, it was now. He was at that age. Been on his own for a few years and starting to feel that tug of wanting a wife and a family before gray hairs set in.

The kids at the orphanage had something to do with that. Anonymously funding a school for orphan children wasn't something he'd ever even thought he'd do. But why not? He had a lot of money, had made a lot of good investments. That's where it all came from. The gambling, not so much. A few hundred here and there, but investing...that's where he'd gotten rich. There was good that could be done with it, which was far better than stuffing it in his mattress and sleeping on it, so why not help children?

The idea had actually come after he'd had dinner one night with his friend, Andrew Radcliffe, over in Spring Falls. He and his wife Evie had founded one. Just before it opened, he toured the school with him, and something felt like it punched him in the gut hard. The rightness of it. The need to do it too.

Andrew and Evie had spent the rest of the evening answering his every question, and helping him get the names of the people he'd need to contact to do something similar. The entire thing took far less time than he'd imagined. Sadly, there were too many orphans out there, and the home was at its capacity fairly quickly.

The hard part had been hiding who he was. The bank had helped, but so had the headmistress. A woman he'd chosen especially. Of course, she could hardly say no, seeing as they were practically family.

Betty Washington had been like a mother to him, when his own was nothing but in her cups. She'd fed him, washed his clothes, and eventually took him in under her roof. He'd owe that woman forever, but she'd never take a bit of repayment, having lost her young son to fever when he was only five, about the same age Kody was when they met.

Though he'd grown up and moved away, like most all young men did to find their own path in life, they'd stayed in constant contact. She'd been a schoolteacher, and Kody gambled, no, he *suspected*, as he was trying not to gamble anymore, she'd not only be perfect to oversee the school, but also delighted.

Luckily for him, he was right.

Even if luck had nothing to do with it. He never misread someone.

Kody cleared his throat. He had to stop thinking like a gambling man. He'd given all that up.

A quick glance at the sky sent him heading in the direction of the school. He needed to check in with Betty, see if she needed anything. He wanted to do that while it was still early afternoon, and the school's interior would be fairly empty.

Though it was unlikely any of the children would care, one or two of the teachers might, and he didn't want to answer questions about what he was doing in the school. It was true, sometimes anonymous donors had their identities revealed, but seeing as the school wasn't even a year old, Kody didn't want that. It was his hope he'd be wrinkles and white haired before it came out.

The sound of children's shrieks of laughter caught his ears, and he drew closer to the school's fence, watching with a grin as he leaned against a tall shade tree. It was good to see so many smiling faces. His heart nearly burst with joy at it.

The odds were already stacked against those kids. If they were to come out on top, or at least somewhere in the middle, they needed a chance and proper education. Someone to point them where to go and help them get there.

Kody frowned as his eyes settled on a young boy. What would life have been like for himself if he'd grown up with two parents? Would he be where he was now? Likely not. But that wasn't a thing to be ashamed of. It was something to think proudly about. After all, had it not been for his rough early years, he wouldn't be where he was now.

He had Betty, and his wits, to thank for that. Though she'd not liked he was a gambling man from an early age, Betty had given him the words of wisdom and the freedom he needed to make his own choices, have his own consequences. That was just what he'd needed. Mistakes made him smarter. Work harder. Be better. All things that got him to where he was now.

Kody's eyes roamed the outside of the school, then he strode toward it. He'd just slip in through the side kitchen door. Maisey the cook knew him and wouldn't question. She thought he did a few repairs now and again about the place. And he had. It was what was needed to sometimes talk with Betty without raising eyebrows.

His hand had just reached for the knob when a woman flickered at the edge of his vision.

"You there!" she called sharply. "What do you think you are doing? This is private property."

Kody ignored her. She looked like the fussy type with her hair in a tight bun, small glasses perched on her nose, and lips pressed in a tight line. She was one of the teachers, likely. Maisey opened the door, saw him standing there and said, "Mrs. Washington isn't here, Mr. Kody." She pushed back a strand of gray hair. "I'm not sure when she'll be back. She's gone to get another child."

"No worries, then," Kody said, continuing to ignore the blonde with venom in her glare quickly approaching. "I'll be back."

He turned, smirking at the gasp of the teacher, who was muttering something under her breath he would have bet—and likely won—wasn't at all polite for children to hear.

Chapter 2

Just as Susan Louden drew close to the kitchen door, the strange man she'd noticed watching the children left. Fury filled her. She knew he'd heard her call out. How dare he pretend he hadn't! There was nothing that infuriated her more than being ignored.

A quick glance at the kitchen door showed Maisey had closed it. The older woman was a little hard of hearing, so likely hadn't heard her. From the vantage point of the door, she wouldn't have seen Susan anyway, so Susan wasn't upset at her. She was furious at the man.

Who just stood around watching children, unless they had some wicked scheme about them? She was well aware that children were snatched, stolen away to be used as hard labor or...Susan swallowed hard, worse. It was her job—no, her duty—to protect these innocent children who had been through so much already. That's why she'd agreed to the teaching position.

Well, that and the fact that she was nearing thirty, and had no prospects whatsoever for matrimony. But that was no one's business but her own.

Susan turned back to the children running over the large yard. One cluster played tag, another with jump ropes. A few boys were kicking a ball back and forth, and two little girls were making dolls from grass. It was a beautiful day, the sky was a bright, cloudless blue, and the golden sun was the perfect temperature. As much as Susan herself longed to stay outside, it was time to resume classes.

"Children," she called, clapping her hands loudly.

Obediently, the children lined up, and followed Susan to the front of the school, where they quietly entered and returned to her classroom. There was a moment's noise as shoes scuffled and chairs scraped while the students settled into their desks.

"Please, open your readers," Susan said, standing before the room, "and practice to yourselves. In a few moments, we will take turns reading."

The shuffling sound of books being pulled out, pages flipped through, and soon the near silence filled her ears as the eight children she taught, from ages seven to nine, studied their readers. Some lips moved silently, some fingers slid along the words, while other children had the skill to read without aid.

Susan walked around the children's small desks quietly, observing them as they read, but frequently her eyes went to the outside, seeking any sign of the man who had been lurking around. Who was he? Why was he there?

He looked slightly familiar, and she wondered if she'd seen him before. Susan pressed her lips together. Surely, if she had, she would have noticed. He was alarmingly handsome. If one could call someone with such a roguish look about him handsome. Thick, dark curls and waves that came to his jaw, eyes that were filled with amusement, strong, broad shoulders that—

Susan clapped the book closed that had been open in her hands, and witnessed each of the children startle. "Forgive me," she said quickly. "My hand slipped. Shall we start? Susie, you will read first, please. Five lines. Go in order."

She moved to the front of the room, trying to focus on the children, not on the man she was irritated with. She had no business even thinking about him. After all, there was the slight possibility that she might be gaining a beau herself. The thought brought the smallest of smiles to Susan's face, and after class ended, her classroom was restored to neatness, and her free time before dinner began, Susan hurried to the small cubby where the mail was kept.

As she sorted through hoping to see her name, disappointment weighed heavily. There wasn't anything. But she squared her shoulders. Perhaps he'd not had time to reply. After all, she'd only mailed her letter three days ago. It usually was a week or more before a reply arrived.

That's why she read his old letters, and had nearly committed them all to memory. There were six, so far.

It had been a bit of a fool's thing to do, when she'd stopped off at the mail-order marriage office that had opened a few months prior. She was curious, more than anything, but before Susan knew it, she'd paid her five-dollar application fee, filled out a form, and had a few gentlemen write to her.

One, though, above all others, had stood out, and that was the man she'd continued to write for the last two months. She felt a little embarrassed, and also uncomfortable that she'd even done such a thing. But his letters...they brought her so much joy. Even if they only had a friendship, that might be enough. It certainly felt nice, as most of her life she'd never been second or third place, but always dead last, as every man she'd ever crossed paths with never looked at her twice.

Perhaps this would be different. She hardly dared hope it would be. After all, the hurts from her past reminded her daily of her physical features' shortcomings. Still, she'd managed to find a measure of happiness on her own. Susan was content being a teacher, and marriage would end that, so she was torn. Her heart wanted both romance and the children. Could she ever have both?

Luckily, this man didn't seem in any hurry to settle down. He'd said as much, and even told her being a teacher was a fine thing, and he wouldn't take her away from that unless it was something she wanted.

"Quite a day, wasn't it, Miss Louden?"

She turned at her name. "Miss Ashe," she answered, smiling at the older woman who taught the children ages ten to twelve. "Yes, the lovely weather makes it hard for children to concentrate on their work," she agreed.

"Did you spot any mail for me?" the other teacher asked.

"I am afraid I wasn't paying any attention," Susan admitted.

"Checking for one from that young man of yours?" Miss Ashe teased.

Susan's cheeks colored, but she managed, "Perhaps."

"If he does get serious, do you think you'll leave us?" the other woman asked. "As I've warned you before, society doesn't let a woman have both a career and a family. You'll have to choose, much as I did."

"I know," Susan sighed, looking off into the distance for a moment. "I want both, though."

"I did too," Miss Ashe said. Then she shook her head. "But I had to choose. And I chose the children. This will be the fifth school I've taught at, and I must say, I like this one best. I feel very fulfilled here, and we teachers are treated in a most luxurious manner! Our own rooms, free time, meals included, a lovely home to live in, a classroom with all we need," she shook her head, "the benefactors are most generous."

Susan agreed. This was only her second teaching position, but it was a far cry from the slapped-together wood building that shook when the wind blew or the door closed too hard. Here, she had eight children, all about the same learning level, compared to the twenty-three ranging from ages five to fourteen.

Miss Ashe was correct in that they were also well treated. The school was large, beautiful, and fully staffed to keep it clean. The teachers focused only on teaching. It was every bit the experience of what one would expect from a private school. Lucky indeed.

Though, the children needed that. Deserved it. They arrived quiet and shocked, some abused and near starving. No matter the child, Mrs. Washington quickly set things to right, and the other children became fast friends.

A small lump came into Susan's throat as she hurried away. One day, perhaps she'd like to be like Mrs. Washington. Running a place such as this. Caring for the children.

But then, what of the man she was fast falling for? Each of his letters held promise that the two of them could be something more than just friends one day.

Though gambling was a sin, and not something she'd ever be a part of, his most recent words had thrilled her and she'd almost, almost, be willing to bet she'd never find another like him. He'd written just what she longed for a man to say. That friendship was enough for now, until *she* was ready.

Susan wasn't sure the answer to when she'd be ready. First, she had to work out how she could have all that she wanted. Because there was one thing that Susan Louden was, and that was a woman who did not compromise.

Chapter 3

"Are you sure?" Kody asked. "The boy's got all he needs?"

"He has now," Betty assured him. "Enough food, clothes that fit, a comfortable bed, and someone to look after him and educate him."

Kody nodded. He leaned forward in the chair before Betty's desk and dropped his head into his hands, before running one through his hair as he looked up at her. "Sometimes, I just wish I could do more."

"You do plenty," Betty told him. "You do more than most. I might not want to know the details of where you got the funds to finance this place, but I can tell you, it's a rare man indeed who cares as much as you do."

"I just want them to be okay," Kody said quietly, around the lump in his throat. "Have someone like you looking after them. Like you did me."

Betty stood and walked around to him. She placed her hand on his shoulder and squeezed it gently. Neither of them said anything. There wasn't anything to say. Not that it was "okay," not that everything would be "all right."

Facts were facts. Life had difficulties, had moments and days and years and even lifetimes of hardships. One had to learn to cope, learn to snatch happiness and manage. Coexist. Even if it was much harder at some times than others.

"What's his name?" Kody asked.

"Josh," Betty said, going back around to her desk. "He's seven."

"And not any family?"

"Not a soul," Betty said with a sigh. "Poor boy doesn't even remember them. It cost a lot to buy him from that man, but worth every penny if you ask me. He wouldn't have lasted much longer there. Thank goodness your friend told us about him."

"I know it," Kody said firmly. "We'll make sure he has a good life." He stood up resolutely. "But let me know if you need anything."

"I will, dear," Betty assured him. "Keep your nose out of trouble," she added.

"Always do." Kody grinned at her. "I'm too slick for trouble to catch me."

"Oh you," she laughed, shaking her head.

Kody left her office, still chuckling to himself. He felt better, knowing there wasn't anything more he could do for the orphanage right now, or for the newest child brought there.

He walked outside and scanned the children playing, curious to see which one was the new boy. It wasn't hard to spot him. A young boy sat nervously on a bench, watching the other children play. Another quick look showed that the annoying woman who had chased after him last time wasn't around, so Kody walked over and sat himself on the opposite side of the bench.

"Hello," he said. "Name's Kody."

The boy glanced at him. "Josh."

"You new here?" Kody asked.

"Third day," the boy answered.

"These people are all right," Kody told him, settling back into the bench. "Matter of fact, Mrs. Washington raised me when I was a boy."

"You an orphan too?" Josh asked.

"Sure am," Kody said. Then, he corrected himself, "Well, was. Mrs. Washington became my family. Just like she and the other kids here will be yours."

"I dunno," the boy answered.

"I do," Kody told him. "I'd bet on it." He gave the kid a grin, and was rewarded with a small one that showed a missing front tooth.

They sat in silence for a minute, then Josh said, "There streams around here? For fishing?"

"Best spot ever," Kody assured him. "You'll get to go there on Sundays. It's a good spot to catch fish, take a nap, or have a little quiet."

"I used to have a place like that," Josh told him. "I liked going there. It was quiet."

"Bet you'll like this place too," Kody said.

He internally scolded himself. Here he was trying to give up thought of gambling, and he'd used the word "bet" twice. And in front of a kid.

Kody was about to say something else, when the school's shrew—he really ought to learn her name—came rushing over.

"You! You! Get off this property," she said, her face bright read and her voice angry.

Josh flinched, and curled into Kody, who wrapped his arm around him. "Hey, you need to calm down," he said, his voice low as he directed a warning look in the woman's direction.

The woman seemed to realize Josh's reaction, and stopped as she looked at the boy.

"I've got to head out," Kody told Josh. "You be okay?" When the boy nodded, he said, "Remember what I said. Mrs. Washington is the best. She'll take good care of you."

"What about you?" Josh asked. "Will I see you again?"

"That would be highly inappropriate," the woman said sharply, "seeing as he doesn't belong here."

Kody ignored her, and winked at the kid. "You can count on it," he told him. "Now, you see that boy there with the green shirt?" When Josh nodded, he said, "You go tell him I want him to show you the best fishing spots on Sunday."

The kid stood, hesitated, then walked over to the other children. He pointed back at Kody, and the other boy nodded, grinning. Kody turned to go, when the woman grabbed his arm.

"Just what do you think you are doing? You cannot just come here and talk to the children. This is private property. And an orphanage."

"I know," he said, looking down at her hand. "I'm trying to leave. Your hand is keeping me here."

"I am not," she gasped, jerking her hand back. Then, she squinted at him. "I've seen you before. At the saloon."

"Oh, you go too?" he asked, crossing his arms with a smirk.

Just like he knew it would, her face turned white, then red again. "Certainly not," she sputtered. "My point is, your type doesn't belong around impressionable children."

"My type?" Kody put on a puzzled look. "What's my type?"

"Gamblers, drinkers, liars, and cheats," she said, raising her chin.

"Well now, I don't drink," he assured her, "and I don't gamble anymore. As for the rest, I might be a liar and a cheat, but I'm a family man at heart."

"So you admit it!" she said, pointing her finger at his chest. "You need to leave before I send for the sheriff."

Kody ignored her last comment as he rubbed at his jaw. It was getting a little scratchy. He might go get a shave next.

"Aren't you going to say anything?" the woman asked again.

He grinned then. He sure was going to say something. "I might have been caught cheating more times than I can count, but I can't count too high. Never had a pretty teacher like you, or maybe I would have learned. Good afternoon, Sunshine."

Kody turned around and walked away, wishing like anything he could see the expression on her face. All the way to the barber he laughed. He hadn't had so much fun teasing someone in a long time.

Chapter 4

Susan scowled as the infuriating man walked away. How dare he speak to her like that? Sunshine? Who called a stranger that? He'd almost been flirting! What they needed was a man on staff. Someone to chase away potential predators. Protect the children.

She glanced over at the children, and was astonished to see Josh now talking with the other boy, large grins on each of their faces. It surprised her because it often took some time before a child felt comfortable enough to make friends here. Not all children were natural extroverts.

Fury filled her at the idea *that man* had helped the boy settle in. He was meddling. A man like that had no business here. None at all.

And...guilt. There was just the smallest bit of guilt that she'd yelled, and startled the boy. She knew better.

Children coming to the orphanage had all experienced some kind of trauma. Many had been abused, and teachers were told from the beginning that they were to be calm, smile, and let Mrs. Washington handle any concerns of a disciplinary situation.

Susan bit her lip. She'd broken that rule, both by shouting, and also by trying to take matters into her own hands, chasing off that man not once but twice. She spun on her heel, determination in her stride as she decided she'd tell Mrs. Washington just what was happening.

Then, she stopped.

Though she liked the headmistress very much, right now all she had was very little that was useful to share. The man's appearance and that he'd been on the property twice, and she'd seen him hanging about the saloon before. There was no evidence of his wrongdoings.

"Then that's what I need to collect," Susan muttered, scowling at the bench where the man had sat so comfortably.

It was also obvious to her that he'd been around a few times, for when Josh had pointed back to him, the other boy, Todd, had brightened up. That didn't sit right with her. Not at all. How many times had that scoundrel been here? Talked to the children?

A thought came to mind just then, and Susan smiled smugly. It didn't matter. He knew she was watching him, and that her eyes would be sharper than ever. In fact, it was likely the last time she'd see that man around. And all for the better. A man like that didn't deserve even an ounce of her attention.

No, the one who did was her sweetheart. Susan took a deep breath and continued back into the school. She'd just returned from the general store and wanted to get her purchases put away.

After climbing the oak staircase to the second floor where the teachers' rooms were, the children being on the third floor, she undid the bundle and pulled out her new package of writing paper.

Though she'd still not gotten a letter from the man she'd been corresponding with, it didn't mean she couldn't write him one.

Susan began her letter, then stopped as the bell for dinner rang. Where had the afternoon gone? She quickly headed to the dining room, where two long tables sat, and stood by her chair as the other teachers, Mrs. Washington, and the students walked in.

Once Mrs. Washington had blessed the food, they ate. There was always an abundance at the school, something she herself appreciated, and knew the students must as well. Mrs. Washington had told her the owner of the school insisted each child be allowed to eat as much as they liked at mealtime, so there was always more than enough to feed them, and something for anyone hungry between meals to beg from the kitchen.

Tonight, as Susan ate her bean soup and cornbread, and listened to the others around her talking quietly, she wondered just who the mysterious benefactor of the school was. She'd never seen them nor heard a name mentioned. When she'd asked, Mrs. Washington had said it was a secret.

None of the other teachers knew, either, and Susan was more than a little curious. While there were homes for other orphans, she doubted many—if any—could match this one in generosity, from the education and basic needs provided, to the comfort in furnishings, food, and quality of caregivers.

Whoever was funding this was a fine individual. She'd like the chance to tell them so herself one day.

The words of the stranger floated through her mind. What was it he'd said? Perhaps if he'd had a teacher as pretty as her to learn his numbers from? She couldn't quite remember, but some of the indignation she had felt had faded. It had been rather nice to be flirted with. Even if he wasn't the sort of person she'd ever be associated with. Susan couldn't recall ever being called pretty.

She knew her features were sharp, and needing spectacles in order to see didn't help things. Truthfully, they made her feel ugly. She didn't know anyone else her age with them.

Maybe he was just flattering her. Likely he was. But there was no harm in letting herself enjoy that for a moment.

She relinquished her soup bowl and plate, and accepted the small dish of custard set before her.

"You seem lost in thought," Miss Ashe said, leaning toward her.

"Do I? I suppose," Susan admitted. "Twice now I've run into a very disagreeable man. I'm hoping there won't be a third time."

"Oh dear," the other teacher answered with a sympathetic look. "I hope not as well. There are far too many of those nowadays, it seems. I am grateful to be here at the school and not living in a large town where there's even more of that sort."

Susan nodded in agreement. Though, she'd never lived by herself before. She'd always lived with her parents, and didn't know what it would be like to be on her own, worried about her safety at night.

The thought made her recall that she owed her mother and father a letter. One had arrived for her a few days ago, and she'd started to reply, and that's when she'd realized she was out of paper. She'd do that tonight.

Her family was not too far away, also living in Kansas, but they had their hands quite full with running the family farm. Though they'd begged her to stay, that wasn't the kind of life Susan wanted. She wanted to see more, do more, and help others.

She felt right here. As though she belonged. A scowl came over her face just then. This was right where she belonged, and she wasn't going to let anyone, even someone with thick, dark curls and a handsome face, keep her from doing her job of teaching and protecting the children.

Chapter 5

Though he had walked away with a smirk, it had long left Kody by the time he got back to his house. A modest, six-room home on the edge of town, it boasted a large kitchen, a sitting room, a private study for him since he was dabbling in not just the orphanage but a few other investments, like partner on a ranch, and three bedrooms.

He wouldn't have built three bedrooms, it just being him and perhaps one day a wife, but he'd bought it, already built, after the town doctor decided to build something a little larger, so that he could have a medical wing on his house.

Sighing deeply, he unlocked the door and walked inside. Josh was on his mind right now. For some reason, he felt worried about the kid. He wasn't sure why he felt that way.

Oh, he'd run off and started talking right away about the fishing, but maybe it was the fact the kid had mentioned a quiet place. Likely meant the boy had a lot on his mind. Kody could relate. Could relate to most all those kids.

Except for he had Mrs. Washington from a young age up, and some of these kids had suffered for a long time without anyone. Thankfully, instead of the mistrust he'd expected, they were settling in well, much to everyone's relief.

Kody settled at the kitchen table with a slab of cornbread covered in honey and a cup of cider. The housekeeper had left him a stew too, but he wasn't hungry enough for that just yet. The smell was enticing, but his stomach was soured from that encounter with the school's teacher. Just what did she think she was doing, talking to him like that? Nasty, that's what she was. Downright nasty. He needed to be sure that she wasn't treating the children like that. They needed love. A firm hand, sure, kids do, but they needed kindness and understanding.

Mrs. Washington knew this. So, why had she hired this woman? He'd need to find out. And learn her name. Perhaps it was just her protective side coming out around the children. He hoped that was it. She was nothing at all like the woman he'd been trading letters with. No, the woman from the letters was warm, intelligent, a little shy but overall sweet and polite. And proper. He couldn't forget proper.

Kody scrubbed his hands over his cheeks and then through his curls. He was trying. Trying to be respectable, and a gentleman. His fingers itched. Not really, more of a feeling that jittered through. He rubbed his hands together and sighed. He had to give it up. Had given it up. But the challenge of winning...it drove him. He relished it.

A horrible thought jolted through him, and Kody sat upright from where he'd slumped back in his seat. Was that why he couldn't stop thinking about that teacher? Was she a challenge? And that's why he couldn't help but tease her or try and get under her skin a little? Maybe he wanted to win her over. That might be the ultimate challenge for a gambler like him.

His smirk returned as he recalled the expression on her face when he'd called her Sunshine. Smoke had nearly poured from her ears. He picked up the newest letter from his mail-order romance. Slowly, the smile faded. The woman writing to him was perfect. Maybe too perfect. It almost unsettled him. She hadn't even pressed for more. Maybe that's part of why his stomach churned. Was he waiting for the bluff from her? Was she bluffing him?

He groaned. He had to remember not everyone was a liar. Not everyone was out to pull one over on him. He shouldn't think that this woman he was writing was.

What he needed was a change of scenery. Something to distract him from these thoughts that had the potential to take over his mind and confuse and frustrate him more.

His eyes roamed the kitchen. He knew Martha had made the stew, but it would keep. What he wanted right now was a chance to talk with a friend or two over a meal. He was going to head to the diner.

The chair scraped loudly as he stood up. Without looking backward, he strode out of the kitchen, and headed right back to town.

The walk there had done him good, and his mood was much lighter by the time he'd gotten to the diner. Along the way, he'd chatted with Carl in front of the general store and let the old man best him in a game of checkers, admired the barber's new hat, and gotten the hankering for one himself. After he'd left there, the sheriff waved to him and asked for his opinion on his new pair of boots.

By the time Kody wandered into the diner and ordered sausages, fried potatoes, beans, and biscuits, along with a tall glass of ice tea, he was feeling back to his normal cheerful self. He chatted here and there with the diner owner and the waitress, and had just picked up his fork to dip it into the pie topped with at least three inches of whipped cream when the diner door opened, and two women walked in.

After a moment's surprise, Kody's smirk was back. It was the teacher. She was with another woman he recognized as another of the teachers at the orphanage. He liked her. She was a grandmotherly sort. Treated the children kindly, and taught some of the older kids. She'd had six of her own, and lost four to illness, and he was sure that's why she made sure not a single one of those children didn't feel parented, to the best of her capability.

"Bart," he said, waving over the diner owner.

"What can I do for you, Kody?" Bart asked. "More to drink? Something different?"

"No, I'm just fine," Kody assured him. "But the two women who walked in are teachers at the orphanage. Put their dinner on my bill, drinks and dessert too."

"Sure thing," Bart told him. "I'll let their waitress know."

He was away before Kody could stop him and tell him to keep it quiet. Oh well. He was sure the one teacher would glare at him when she found out, but he didn't care. He wasn't doing it for her, so much as the other teacher. Kody's fork slipped into the pie, and he grinned. Or was he? Maybe this was part of his gamble. The challenge. Getting a smile from Sunshine.

Or at least to have her treat him like a decent human being.

The meal was set before the two women, and several bites had been eaten when the waitress mentioned their meal and dessert was paid for. Sure enough, a storm cloud formed over the younger teacher's face, and Kody felt the grin growing on his.

The women stood and walked to his table.

"Ladies." Kody smiled.

"You are too generous," the older teacher said, beaming at him. "Thank you, dear boy."

Kody wished he could remember her name. He puzzled it over while the other teacher shook her head.

"It's not needed," the rude one said, her voice harsh. "We don't need anything from you."

"Then you don't have to accept it," Kody said, fighting the laugh that wanted to rumble forth from her expression. "But I think it's a little late to give it back, and Bart doesn't give refunds, so I'm not sure what you'll do about that."

The woman sputtered, and glared at him, but the older teacher, he remembered her name now, Mrs. Lucas, giggled. "Oh you! Thank you, dear! We appreciate it." And then she pulled the first teacher away, half dragging her back to the table.

Kody tried not to watch as she picked at the dessert set out, before giving in to the luscious cream and berry concoction. He stood. Though he'd love nothing more than to stick around and catch the glares she was sending his way, he had something else to do.

Write a letter to the woman who did like his attentions.

Chapter 6

"I'll see you back at the school," Mrs. Lucas said, waving a hand at Susan. "I'll just be stopping by the dressmaker before I go. I'm hoping that she's got my new underthings ready, and save her delivery boy a trip to the school."

"Yes, of course," Susan said. "Take your time. I have an errand to run myself. I'll see you soon."

After their dinner—which she had been enjoying until she'd discovered *that man* had provided it—Susan was glad to have a few moments by herself to try and regain her temper. She wasn't quite sure why it had upset her so. Mrs. Lucas had been delighted at the meal and the dessert. And Susan had to admit it had been delicious, and a wonderful treat. Neither of the women would have ordered a dessert, both being of a mind to avoid the appearance of luxury.

But she just didn't like the fact that he had taken it upon himself to do that. Something about it galled her. Who was he, thinking he could take such liberties every place he went? He didn't own the town. He was a gambler, a cheat, a liar.

Smoke just about poured out of her ears, she was so steamed. And once alone, she felt a bit like a liar and a criminal as she slunk around the town, looking out for the man. A liar, because she didn't really have an errand. Unless you could call spying on someone or trying to get more information about them an errand. And guilty, because this wasn't like her at all. She'd never done anything like this in her life.

Still, Susan justified it by saying she was sure that he was up to no good. Here, in town, and with him nearby, it was the perfect time to prove it. So, she'd just tuck those feelings she was wrestling with away, and move forward with purpose, as that was what was needed.

After almost an hour, and with no sign of the man she'd seen far too much for her liking, Susan squared her shoulders and slowly walked past the one place she'd been avoiding. A place filled with sin. Swearing, gambling, a smoky haze, and scantily clad women. A den that what she was sure was filled with the worst kind.

The *saloon*.

Her lips pressed in a tight line, and every bit of her tensed as she walked toward the tall building, where tinkly piano music spilled out in a disgustingly cheerful sound. Though the saloon was supposedly well maintained, and there weren't too many fights that she'd heard of, Susan was sure it was a place that shouldn't even exist.

She walked past slowly, trying not to stare inside, but all the same looking for the unknown man.

"Help you find someone?" an old man asked.

Susan startled. She'd been so busy looking, she hadn't noticed anyone nearby her.

"Ahh, well," she hesitated, taking in the small man, the large hat perched on his head and dust-covered boots up on a barrel, then suddenly said, resolutely, "I've seen a man around the orphanage where I work. Tall, dark curly hair. I wondered who he was. If he was a danger to the children, I mean. Not personally wondering. As I happened to be walking past, I was trying to see if I spotted him around."

Susan was sure she was stammering, and just hoped she made sense. Her cheeks were hot with embarrassment.

The old man shook his head. "Naw. No chance of that. Not seen him here for a while. Don't gamble no more. A shame." The man pointed to his hat and grinned. Susan noticed a few missing teeth. "See this? Bought me a new one after a shootout, and the old one took a bullet."

Susan gasped, and one hand flew to her lips. "That could have been your head!"

"Yep. Coulda. Don't get myself into those situations anymore. Gave up the drink and the cards. See how I'm outside? If'n he can change, I can too. That's right, I said, 'Carl, even an old codger like you can do new things and be a better person.' The missus is right proud of me."

"I...see. Yes. Of course."

"But that boy? Naw, he ain't here. He's sitting pretty now, got more money than he can spend in a lifetime. Got his fingers in this business and that one." Carl waved his arms around wildly. "Likes to spread it around. Help others. You know when the church roof blew off and the sheriff's office had its winders broke from that storm a few months ago? That was him that done paid for the repairs. Not the townsfolk. Maybe that's why he's there at your school. Who don't have a soft spot for a tyke? 'Specially one with no folks. Maybe he's donating."

That wasn't what Susan had expected to hear at all. In fact, it left her wordless. How did one answer that? The man was a do-gooder? It was hard to believe.

The saloon door swung open, and a man stumbled out. He reeked of liquor and sweat and something else she didn't want to guess at. An older woman approached the man, and the look of sadness in her eyes as she wrapped an arm around him and led him away sent Susan spiraling into the past. The other woman's expression was too familiar. She'd seen it many times on her grandmother's face.

Nodding her thanks at the man, she hurriedly left, before she was seen talking to someone in front of the saloon. It didn't matter that it was an old man. It was the fact that she'd been standing in front of a place that wasn't the least bit reputable, she was a woman, and she was a teacher.

On her walk back to the orphanage, she had an argument with herself. Part of her was trying to convince herself that the man she'd seen at the school was of little threat, if any. In fact, she felt a little bit guilty after hearing the man—and she'd forgotten to ask his name—sounded like he was good. Kind and thoughtful and trying to turn his life around. Even inspiring others to as well.

If he'd paid for the storm damages, repaired the church roof, surely the pastor must think him a good man. Otherwise, he wouldn't have allowed such a thing, right? Was she being too judgmental?

But maybe she wasn't. A larger part of her knew that just because someone wanted to change didn't mean that they would or even could. Change was hard. She'd seen that firsthand, when her grandfather had tried many times over the years to stop drinking. He'd not been able to, and it had driven him to an early grave. Along the way, he'd lost friends, distanced himself or driven away family, and even harmed himself.

Was that...was that why she was worried about the strange man with the captivating eyes and the thick curls? She didn't want anything to happen to him? Susan scoffed, and quickly dismissed that idea the second it crossed her mind. No, that wasn't it at all.

Her concern was over the children's safety. He'd been watching the children. That man was up to something, and she was going to put a stop to it, before it got far enough to hurt anyone.

Chapter 7

"I'm so glad you were able to come over," Kody's friend Grace said, squeezing his hand in greeting.

"Thank you for inviting me," Kody told her, nodding a hello at Grace's children, a teenage girl and a young boy. "Something smells real good."

"That might be my cobbler," Alice said. "It's Pa's favorite, so I hoped you'd like it too."

"I'm sure I will," he told her with a smile.

"James should be up any moment," Grace said. "Have a seat."

Kody settled into a spot at the kitchen table and watched as Calvin, who was growing taller each time he saw him, sat across from him, whittling away on a soft piece of wood that was slowly turning into an animal of some kind. He was glad to see the kids settling in.

Grace had been a widow, trying to raise her two children on her own before James came around. A former gunslinger, he'd actually answered an advertisement to help her in the store and stop break-ins that had been occurring. One thing led to another, and James—who neither Kody nor James thought would ever settle—ended up falling head over heels for Grace, and her children who adored him with all of their beings.

Footsteps on the stairs leading from the general store they owned and lived over top of sounded, and Kody stood, grinning as he clasped James's hand. "How are you?" he asked.

"Better every day," James said. "I highly recommend the family life. I thought I had it all before, but now I know I do."

A pang hit Kody, right in the chest, but he ignored it. After all, wasn't that why he was corresponding with a woman? He might be having the same one day. Maybe he'd even have a kid or two calling him pa. That didn't sound too bad.

Grace was a fine cook, and filled his belly until near bursting. Alice had plied two large helpings of blackberry cobbler on him, and after dinner, Grace and the children had left, going downstairs to work on the store inventory, leaving him and James alone for some conversation. He appreciated that. Something was weighing on him, this whole situation with the teacher at the school, and he wondered if James might be able to set his mind at ease any.

"You look good," Kody said. "The kids seem so happy. Grace too."

"They are, and it makes me glad. It wasn't easy to get here." James looked down into his mug thoughtfully. "I made some mistakes because I didn't know what I was doing, but I'm glad it worked out. Hardest thing was putting pride aside."

"That's always a difficult thing," Kody agreed.

Was pride part of what was driving him toward his actions each time he teased that young teacher? Or was it something else? It wasn't attraction. No way it was that. She wasn't his kind of woman at all, and it was beyond obvious that he wasn't the type of man she'd ever like.

"Something's bothering you," James said quietly. "Anything I can do to help? We can ride out together and be back before sunrise if it's that kind of a problem, and not too far away. If it's further away, Grace will understand, and we can leave in the morning with the sun. The gunbelt might not be used as often, but I'm not rusty."

"I appreciate it, but it's not that kind of problem." Kody sighed. "That's the easy sort. Problems in the saloon are easy. No, it's just I'm having a hard time escaping the past. Preconceived notions. Expectations. I thought it'd be easy to start over, but it's not. It's hard because people don't ever let you forget what you do. What you did."

"I get that," James said, leaning back in the chair and crossing one ankle on his knee. "While I help the sheriff now and again, he forgets at times I'm not a gunslinger anymore."

"It's come in handy, though," Kody said. "Gambling doesn't."

"Not true," James argued. "You've learned a lot from your time at the card table. You see people. Read them. That's a valuable tool. Don't forget all of the money you've won, a lot of it from cheats, and you've put it to good. Done a lot of things to help people."

"That's all true," Kody admitted. "But tonight, watching you and Grace and the kids, it made me wonder if I'll ever get a little bit of that. Family. I've not had one in so long, and mine wasn't like this. I'm scared maybe I'm too broken for one."

"Well, you can't have Grace," James laughed, "but I might give you Calvin. He's a handful. Better than he was, but still a handful."

"Weren't we all at that age?" Kody chuckled. "Alice seems like she's calming down."

"She is," James said. "Though there are days I'd give you her too." He shook his head. "I can't tell you how stressful being a parent is. I've got to hand it to Grace. She's an amazing woman, raising those two on her own for so long.

I couldn't have done that myself. I still don't know how she did it."

"Takes a skill beyond my own," Kody agreed. "Mrs. Washington did that for me, and I'll be forever grateful. She manages that orphanage and those kids like she was born for it. Me? I feel like I'm stumbling around sometimes when I'm talking to them, not sure the right thing to say."

"The more you are around them, the easier it gets," James told him. "Kids and women. Anyone caught your eye?"

"I'm not sure. Maybe," Kody said. "I've been writing someone. Not met her yet. She's all right, though. Sounds nice."

"But?" James asked.

"But she seems real refined. Classy."

"Not the kind of woman for a guy like you?" James raised his brows.

"That's what it feels like. And like I'm holding my breath. Wondering if she finds out about the real me, what's going to happen. I'm almost... I don't know." Kody shrugged and shook his head.

"Afraid to get your hopes up?" James asked.

"That might be it," he agreed. "There's another woman I've crossed paths with a few times. A teacher at the orphanage. She looks at me like I'm something stuck to the bottom of her shoe."

"Ouch," James winced.

"I reckon I'm worried if she's that disgusted with me, and we don't even know each other, what chance have I got with a woman like the one I'm writing to? Eventually we are going to meet. Maybe I ought to stop this before it gets too far. Not that we've been rushing. Don't have any plans, really. Just thinking out loud."

"Sounds like a tough thing," James told him. "Been there myself."

"Any advice?" Kody asked, not even letting himself be embarrassed he was asking.

"Lots of it. Be yourself. Always. You're a good person. Don't let anyone tell you otherwise. That woman, if she's the one for you, she'll see that. And if she's not, then you'll find the right one."

James seemed so sure of himself, and Kody nodded, letting the words sink in, but as Calvin burst through the door, seeking help on his arithmetic he'd just remembered he had to do, Kody felt those pangs again, and couldn't help but hope his friend was right. He wanted a wife, a family. Someone to surround himself with, and give the love he knew he had in him to share.

The question was, was he willing to gamble on this woman he'd been writing to?

Chapter 8

"Make me a list," Mrs. Washington told each of the teachers, "One hundred dollars each of supplies or books for your classroom. Whatever you think you'd like the children to have."

"My goodness," Susan said, glancing about to see the other teachers also with wide eyes. "What's the occasion?"

"Our benefactor has made another donation," Mrs. Washington said. "He's tasked me with finding out if there are any additional needs, and to also bolster the clothing supply closet. I suspect he might have gotten wind of a child or two who may need to join us soon."

"But so much!" one of the teachers said.

"Likely a drop in the bucket to him," Susan said. "The way this place looks." When the others looked at her, she stammered, "I mean, not that I'm not grateful. The children are so well cared for. I was comparing to the school I was at previously."

"This school is little like others," Mrs. Washington said. Her voice had grown stern. "Here, we don't just provide a bare education, scanty food, and worn clothing. We nurture."

There were murmurs of agreement from the others. "He's a good man," Mrs. Washington continued. "We are fortunate to have him."

"Indeed," Susan said, her head lowered as mortification filled her face.

Once again, she wondered who it might be. Who was wealthy enough to fund such a place?

"We ought to have him for dinner one night," Ms. Ashe said.

Susan startled. "Do you mean that he lives nearby?"

Mrs. Washington held up a hand. "He wishes to keep his identity quiet, for now. But, yes."

Susan's mind started to sort through the people that she knew in the town. The town had a few wealthy men, ranchers, business owners, but none that she'd ever heard connected with philanthropy on the scale of the size of the school. Which was odd, now that she thought about it.

Usually, men of great wealth liked to make sure their names were attached to charitable activities. They'd give, but they'd be sure everyone knew it was them who did so.

Usually, it was the simpler folks who kept quiet when they donated, but an average person didn't have this kind of money. Susan couldn't even fathom just how many tens of thousands of dollars this school cost to build and run. So, who would have this kind of money?

As she turned the names over in her thoughts, a face sprang to her mind. Eyes that were filled with mirth, dark, curly hair just begging to have fingers run through it, and—

She stiffened. What was she thinking?

Mrs. Washington's voice broke through her thoughts. "A generous man. He has an understanding of what it's like to be an orphan and a child who is neglected. Because of that, he has a great empathy toward these children and wants to make sure that they have every advantage he can offer them."

As the teachers listened on quietly, Mrs. Washington added, "I foresee many—if not all—of these children growing up and doing great things, thanks to him." She wiped at a tear, then added, "It's my greatest desire to assist in their growth and development, and be worthy of the trust he's placed in me."

Susan felt a lump in her throat as well, and moisture in her eyes. She'd always taken her role as a teacher seriously, but somehow, it had never crossed her mind that by being here, she was making a difference. It was clear that Mrs.

Washington trusted her, and that the man who had built and paid for everything trusted her.

Who was he? Could it possibly be the man who had been at the orphanage? Perhaps that's why she'd seen him here. He was making a donation, checking on things. Checking on the newest arrival. That would explain, too, why he'd been talking to the boy.

Susan closed her eyes as she exhaled deeply. If it was him, had she made a terrible mistake in being rude to him at the diner? But he hadn't seemed upset. He'd been mocking, teasing, as he was each time. Which infuriated her greatly.

But it also intrigued her. How was it he never got upset? She'd all but verbally attacked him.

Nervously, she twisted the necklace at her throat as she listened to Mrs. Washington.

"...on my desk by the end of tomorrow, please." Mrs. Washington smiled. "I wish to place the order for what you need as soon as possible."

Susan nodded, intending to make her list that evening. Her mind spun through the possibilities. New books, yes. The children loved stories. Perhaps some new pencils, paper. They could have ample to create their own books. One hundred dollars. It was an enormous amount, on top of the already well-stocked classroom.

"What will you ask for?" Miss Ashe asked, coming over to her.

"I'm not sure yet. Books, papers, pencils. That's as far as I've gotten," Susan said. "What of you?"

"The same," Miss Ashe said. "Along with paints and some canvas. We have been studying Italian painters. Perhaps the children would like to try that themselves."

"What an idea," Susan mused. "It is a good one. Indeed, there can be no finer orphanage than this one."

Mrs. Washington came up to her just then, and placed her hand on Susan's arm. "We try not to call this place an orphanage," she reminded her. "It is simply a school, and a home for whatever boys and girls need it."

"Yes, ma'am," Susan quickly said, ashamed she'd made two mistakes in front of the headmistress. It was a wonder she still had her job. "I'm sorry."

"There's no need to be," Mrs. Washington said with a warm smile. "A slip of the tongue. It's just the children have been through so much, that we want to avoid reminding them that they are without biological parents, if we can. Here, we are all family."

"I understand," Susan said.

The headmistress walked away, and Susan glanced at her thoughtfully. Would Mrs. Washington ever tell who the school's mysterious benefactor was? The question now not only burned in her, but made her near desperate to know, especially if it was the man who she'd seen.

But that evening, as she made out her list for the additional supplies she would like—including watercolors for her class—Susan shook her head. No, it wasn't that man. He had a past. He was a gambler. Men like that wouldn't do anything as good as this. They cared about one thing. More gambling.

Susan was convinced that not only was that man a scoundrel, but he also wasn't the school's benefactor. Now, she just needed to figure out who he was. She had two mystery men right now to think about.

Just then, her eyes fell to the newest letter from the man she'd been writing. Three, if she counted him. And she could. She'd never met him before. Knew only what he'd written.

A small laugh escaped her. Never in her life would she have thought her mind would be torn between wondering about three different men. She should only be thinking about the man she was writing, but something about those laughing eyes and dark curls kept drawing her thoughts to the unnamed man.

Susan pressed her lips together, and scowled. How dare he. He had no right. No right to be at the school, no right to tease her, and no right to be on her mind constantly. It was another black mark against him.

Chapter 9

Kody stifled a yawn as he pushed open the diner's door. He waved to the waitress, then pointed to a seat near a window. When she nodded, he sat, and rubbed his hands over his face. It had been a long day.

First, he'd had a pile of contracts to read through with his lawyer. Everything from updates to the ranches he invested in to legalities with the orphanage, a contract to hire two new teachers and a handyman, stableman, and three men to help in in a few months, and then for builders, to add on a small barn on the school property.

Kody had the idea to have old, docile horses and ponies, and have the children not only learn to ride, but also to care for them, to saddle or hitch them, and be familiar with them as it could be a valuable job skill. With the handyman, he was hoping to find one who had a passion for helping others and patience in abundance, as learning those kinds of skills might also benefit some of the boys.

He didn't need more teachers, yet, but Mrs. Washington had the idea of perhaps teaching some of the older students, if they were so inclined, how to become a teacher. One of the women was also exceptional in needlework, another valuable skill that could be taught.

Once the children were nearing adulthood, Kody knew it would be important to help them find jobs, to see they were in good situations. He knew that one of the boys and two of the girls were curious about working in medical care. It was his goal to see if the town doctor would consider letting them help him, and learn if that was something they'd want to go to college for one day. If it was, Kody was determined to find a way to support them.

But there was so much to think about and do and coordinate. It was a little more than he'd realized when he opened the place, though he wouldn't have it any other way.

"Here you are," the waitress said, dropping off a cup of coffee and a slice of cherry pie. She looked at him sympathetically. "You look tired."

"I am," Kody answered, grabbing the mug. "Not the body, but the mind. Thank you. I hadn't even ordered yet, but this will hit the spot."

She nodded. "It's from the woman in the corner, by the way."

Surprised, Kody looked to where she indicated. There, the teacher from the school was looking at him nervously. The waitress walked away, and the woman stood, hesitating only a moment before throwing her shoulders back and crossing toward him.

Before Kody could stand, she was there. "I'm sorry," she said. "I've been rude. Especially if you are who I think you are, and for that I'm more than sorry."

He stared at her curiously. "Have a seat," he offered, nodding to the chair across from him. "Just who do you think I am?"

The woman seemed to steel herself, then nodded briskly, and pulled out the chair across from him. "I think you are—" she stopped, and lowered her voice—"I think you are the man responsible for the school of orphans. And, by default, the one who pays me to teach there."

Kody didn't answer. He took a bite of his pie to stall for time. How had she figured that out? It made him feel better, that she'd apologized for being rude, but it also made him wonder, was she doing it simply because she was worried about his keeping her employed?

He studied the woman before him carefully. She was nervous. He could tell. Her lips were tight, her eyes darting around, her hands beneath the table. Clasped, or fidgeting, he was willing to bet, and her chest was hardly moving, so Kody had the feeling she was so tense that she was barely able to breathe.

"Are you going to say something?" she asked, her voice slightly shrill. "Or just stare at me?"

He smiled, and took another bite of the pie. When he'd swallowed, he said, "I'm not sure yet, Sunshine. What do you want me to say? Other than thank you for the pie and the coffee. It's appreciated."

"That...that..." She was quiet, and then bristled. At the nickname she didn't like or his words, he wasn't sure. Finally, she said, "I don't know."

"Tell me," Kody said, sitting back and crossing his arms over his chest. "If I was that man, would it change your low opinion of me? And why?"

The woman stilled, and her head lowered. When she met his eyes a moment later, her voice was low. "Yes. Because I made a mistake." She took a deep breath. "I was hired to help care for these children. That's what I thought I was doing, by keeping a stranger, and someone I discovered was a gambler, away from them."

He studied her a moment, then drank from his mug. "I understand that," he told her as he picked back up the fork.

"Then?"

"Then what?" Kody asked.

"I've apologized. What will you do? Send me away for my foolishness?"

"Why would I do that?" Kody asked. "If I did, the children would be losing out on a good teacher. One who cares about them deeply."

Her cheeks flushed slightly, and Kody marveled at how she was almost pretty, when she flashed a small smile at him. "Thank you," she said quietly, as she pushed her small spectacles up her nose. "I do." There was silence for a moment, and then she asked, hesitation filling her voice, "Do you mind if I ask something?"

"Go ahead."

She rested her hands on top of the table, clasping them. "What interest do you have in these children? You do so much for them. It's...it's not like anything I've ever seen or heard of before. Honestly, it amazes me. You do all of this," she waved her arm in a wide gesture, "but keep quiet about it."

He nodded slowly. What she said was true. But was he willing to share his secret with her? The woman's face was honest. Open. He felt he could trust her.

"I'm an orphan," he finally said. "But before I was one, my early years were not the kind I'd wish on any child."

Her eyes were locked onto his. Kody wanted to stop, didn't want to see the judgment he was sure would be there if he kept talking, but he did it anyway.

"My father wasn't a good man, and when he left, I wasn't sad at all. My mother couldn't take her lips off a bottle of liquor long enough to even notice I was around, until the bottle was empty. Then she'd beat me."

There was a gasp, but Kody ignored it. "Luckily, I learned to run fast, and how to hide, so that happened less. I lived off whatever food I could steal or dig up from a neighbor's garden, but I was nearly always starving."

Had his voice cracked? He wasn't sure. His heart was aching. Not so much because of his past, but because he knew too many kids suffered the same as he had, only he hadn't found them yet to protect them. Help them.

"One day, she didn't come home from the store. Found out later, she'd been run over by a wagon. Mrs. Washington... Betty, she was the neighbor I'd been stealing from for a while. I guess she knew it too. She watched me digging up a carrot, and told me it would taste better in a stew. She brought me into her house, fed me. Gave me clothes. We talked a little, and realized we had something in common. I was a boy without a mother, and she was a mother without a boy.

"From that day on, she took care of me. Fed me, clothed me, educated me. Always told me I had value, I could do anything I set my mind to."

Kody looked off into the distance through the window and watched as a family walked past. He nodded toward them, and said, "I never had that. But I knew I wanted to help the others who were like me. And I knew there wasn't another soul out there I could trust more than her to help me. We might not be able to save every child, though I sure wish we could, but I do sleep better at night, knowing that maybe I can make a difference for some of them."

After a long moment, Kody dragged his eyes to the woman's face, and was surprised to see a tear tracking down her cheek. "Hey, Sunshine," he said softly, leaning forward and brushing his thumb over the moisture. "Don't waste those on me."

"I don't know what to say," she said quietly.

"I understand not everyone likes my past. And I admit, I'm not proud of all of it, and that's why I try to do good." Kody reached for his mug but saw it was empty, and set it down.

"You've nothing to apologize for," the woman murmured.

"I don't know," Kody mused. "I've been writing a woman. Won't lie. I'm scared when she finds out what kind of a man I really am, how I grew up, she'll say goodbye. Not that we were real serious yet or anything, but there's two kinds of women out there. The ones who accept a man with a questionable past and those who don't. I get the feeling she's the second kind."

Kody looked out the window again, but almost startled when a warm hand rested on his. A strange feeling filled his belly as he looked at the slim fingers resting on his.

"Then that woman would be a fool," the teacher said quietly.

Chapter 10

Several of the children stood on small spots marked out on the lawn. One held a baseball bat, and squinted at the pitcher. A tall, handsome man with thick curls, calling out encouragement to the batter.

Susan tried not to stare, but she couldn't help it. He seemed so at ease with the children, and every single one of them seemed to adore him. Something in her had changed, since she'd bought the man his pie and coffee, and heard his story. She also almost, *almost*, didn't mind him calling her Sunshine.

She didn't know why she'd bought him that pie, or even why she spoke with him other than to apologize. That hadn't been her intention at all. Yet, he'd looked so exhausted, so concerned, something made her do it. And, just as quickly, had made her realize that perhaps she was wrong, and he was the school's founder. It was obvious that he carried a great weight on his shoulders. It had turned out, she was right. His burdens were far more than she could have ever imagined. Last night, she'd lain late into the night thinking about him.

And, how once again, she'd forgotten to ask his name. She'd have to remember the next time she saw him, though by that point it was going to feel quite awkward when she did.

Someone's shadow fell across her, and she glanced over at Mrs. Washington.

"So, you know about him," the headmistress said quietly.

"Yes," Susan said. "But I won't tell a soul. You have my word."

The older woman simply nodded. "I trust you. He must also, if he shared that information. My boy is good. But he doesn't want to take credit or call attention to himself for helping others. He does it because it needs to be done. Not for ego's sake."

They stood in silence, watching the child with the bat swing and miss, then swing and miss again. On her third try, the bat tapped the ball, and everyone cheered for the little girl as she started to run toward a base.

Susan clapped for the child, then turned to say something, but saw Mrs. Washington was gone. Just as well. She wouldn't have to make polite conversation. She could think.

Think about how she was in a terrible situation. It hadn't been her intention, not at all, but ever since that day in the diner last week, Susan's mind had been constantly thinking about one person. Him.

And she didn't even know his name. How ridiculous was that? It had crossed her mind to ask, but two things had stopped her. The first, that if she did, and he'd already told her, she'd seem a fool. The second, that if she learned it, it made him more *real*.

Something she didn't want. Couldn't have. Why, she was all but promised to the man she had been corresponding with. What on earth would he think about her? It would be a poor opinion indeed. Susan was determined that her thoughts would remain nothing but curious. Friendly.

But each time she looked at his smile, heard his laugh, her stomach fluttered. He was a good man. She saw that now. Worst of all, he was a man who she felt a spark of attraction to. What was she to do? This excitement that filled her when he glanced her way, the tingles she still got when she remembered his fingers accidentally brushing against hers, absolutely haunted her.

Then, the way he called her Sunshine...it wasn't always sarcastic. When his thumb had brushed her cheeks, his touch had been as gentle as his tone.

Guilt filled her every pore. But what about her potential beau? While, no, she wasn't engaged, she had still been writing with intention. Did that make her thoughts, as innocent as she tried to keep them, a sin?

And, why would she even be interested in someone like him? A man like that, handsome, teasing, wealthy...he wasn't the sort to notice someone like her. Not in the way she'd like. He was likely just being kind. Besides, he'd mentioned he had his own woman he'd been writing.

Susan clenched her fists, and tried to stop the tears that burned suddenly. What was wrong with her? Why was she upset?

But she knew. Had known it from the moment he'd looked into her with those eyes filled with pain. She felt something for this man. Him. Not the one she'd been writing. And, she was jealous. She didn't even know his name, but she knew she loathed that another woman had his attention, even if it was just by letter. She was a fool, too, if she didn't end up falling for him. Questionable past or not.

Breathing in sharply, she turned and strode toward the school. She needed to remove herself from temptation. Focus her attention on the man who had her interest first.

A few moments later, Susan was clutching a letter in her hand from her sweetheart that had just arrived in the mail. It was all she could do to get to a quiet place to read it. The school library was close by, so that's where she went.

The room was large and filled with chairs, small tables, thick carpets, a tall fireplace, and books. Many, many books. They rested on shelves that stretched just above her head and lined two walls. There was a wealth in here, both in stories and facts, and the room was a favorite of each student.

Susan took herself to one of the chairs next to a window and carefully opened the letter. As she read it, dread filled her. Then guilt, again. Finally, fear.

"What will I do?" she whispered, as she reread the letter.

Miss Ashe walked into the room and gasped. "Why, my dear! You look as though you've had the most terrible of news. Whatever is wrong?"

With trembling fingers, Susan refolded the letter and whispered, "The man I've been writing. He...he wants to meet me."

"But isn't that good?" Miss Ashe asked. "That must mean he is quite serious about you."

Susan didn't answer. If she met this man, then he became real. Would have expectations. What was she to do? Should she agree to meet him? He wasn't clear in his letter, saying why he wanted to, only that he did, and it was urgent. Did urgent mean he wished to propose? Perhaps he was tired of their relationship being on paper?

A shriek from outside caught her attention, and she looked through the window to see the baseball game, its pitcher still there, making sure each child had a turn.

Susan closed her eyes and drew in a shuddering breath. The moment had come, and she had to face a very alarming truth. She was falling in love with the man whose name she still didn't know, and she was no longer interested in—perhaps—the only man in the world who would want a woman such as her.

Chapter 11

Kody shoved his hands into his pockets as he strolled away from the post office. He'd been hoping for a letter from the woman he'd been writing. After he'd unexpectedly shared his past with the teacher at his school, he realized something. She'd been on his mind nonstop.

Worse, he had the suspicion that he might actually like her. For a solid day, he'd tried to convince himself that wasn't it. It was the thrill of a challenge. Getting that win. Acing the bet.

But the truth was, that wasn't it. There was something in her, something she wasn't telling anyone, that spoke to him. Pulled him in. That, and her obvious desire to protect the children there at the school.

But what did that mean for him? And the woman he'd been writing? Part of being a new man was being honest.

With himself, with others, and even when it was hard and he didn't really want to.

And that meant being honest with the woman he'd been writing. He had to see her. Had to know if there was a spark, or if she thought any one way or another about him. Had to figure this out—figure them out—because if he couldn't, he was going to end up in a mess if he started following his head instead of his heart.

Taking in a deep breath, Kody slowly released it, trying to let some of the stress over the situation leave him.

"Howdy, Kody!" Carl called from the general store.

"Good to see you," Kody said, pausing before the old man.

"There was a woman looking fer ya," Carl told him. "Tall, thin, had spectacles."

Kody nodded. "She found me."

"Looked fiery," Carl said. Then, he leaned in closely. "Weren't I a happily married man..." He winked, and grinned, showing his missing tooth.

With a laugh, Kody patted him on the shoulder. "If you weren't a married man, you'd have your pick," he assured Carl.

He gave a wave and continued down the street. That woman. Couldn't escape her anywhere. And the most infuriating part? It was that he didn't even know her name! Of course, today wasn't the first time he'd mused over that, wondered what it was.

Ethel. Carlotta. Beatrice.

She could be anything. But she sure wasn't Sunshine. Did the woman ever smile? He laughed and shook his head. Why did it matter to him?

His stomach clenched, and Kody knew it wasn't from his lunch. It was because he was attracted to the woman. For some reason, though she riled up his every nerve, she also set him ablaze with desire. It wasn't just the want, the need, to win at a gamble. It wasn't even to puzzle her out, though he'd have liked that too.

No, it was to spend more time with her. See her smile. Make sure she never shed another tear.

Kody felt his chest tighten. She'd cried. Over him. Had anyone ever done that before? He didn't think so. It had...it had meant far more than she'd likely ever know.

He swallowed hard. That's why he had to do the right thing. For her. For himself. For the woman he had been writing. He had to see if he and the teacher had anything between them. It had been tempting to make the decision by letter. Tell the woman he'd been writing he was no longer interested. Make up some excuse. Like, he had to leave town. Was no longer wanting marriage. But that wouldn't have been right to do to her. Heck, wouldn't have been right to do to himself. She might have turned out to be something special.

Regardless, Kody had to be upfront. Something like a parting of ways needed to be done in person. Softly. Kindly.

Writing the letter and asking her to meet him had been one of the most difficult things he'd ever done. Kody didn't like the idea of leading a woman on if he wasn't interested in her. The problem was, he didn't know if he was or not. And the teacher...he knew something was there. He owed it to himself and the woman he'd been writing, and the teacher, to see where the future might lead.

He stopped before his house, and once he let himself in, locked the door and leaned his forehead against it.

There was a terrible pain in his chest. Kody knew what it was, too. For so long, he'd been alone. Felt unwanted. Like someone no one could love. Would want to love. The truth was, that still likely was the truth. That teacher's kindness, the compassion in her eyes and words, they'd been for the situation. Not for him.

But they'd stirred up something. Woke the desire to be loved. To have love. And Kody knew he had to have it now, and if he was rejected by the woman his heart was wanting, then he'd just have to try and win her over. He'd played tougher hands before, and was willing to bet it all for this one.

Suddenly, his hands acted of their own accord, as one yanked open the front door. Kody found himself back on the street, heading toward the school.

"What am I doing?" he asked. "This is stupid."

There was no answer. He hadn't really expected there to be, and Kody tried to get his thoughts in order before he arrived at the school.

All too soon, he'd arrived there, and stared at the large building and grounds. As always, pride filled him, as well as responsibility. Today, though, he wasn't there to see the school. He was there to see the woman he just couldn't get out of his mind.

Kody went around to the kitchen door, and let himself in. Maisey gave him a smile.

"I'm just going to pop in," he told her.

"Stop by for a few of these warm oatmeal cookies before you go," Maisey told him.

With a grin and a nod, Kody went through the door to the main hallway. It was deserted, as were the front rooms. Kody glanced at a large clock. Of course. The children would be in their lessons.

Just as soon as he thought that, a bell rang, and the sound of dozens of shoes filled his ears, as the children streamed in excited, though orderly lines.

Josh passed him, and gave a solemn nod. Kody's chest squeezed a little as he nodded back. A moment later, the teacher he'd been searching for passed him, then stopped, her eyes wide as she realized he was standing there.

"Hello," he told her.

"Hello," she whispered.

"I want to talk to you," he told her. "I know now isn't a good time. This evening, maybe?"

She bit her lip, and he found his eyes drawn to them. "Yes. That would be fine. Perhaps seven?"

"Sure. How about the bench by the kitchen? Then it's still proper. You don't have to worry about what people might think," he said, giving her a crooked grin, even if he hated the truth of his words.

Josh came into the hall, and stopped short as he saw them.

"Go outside," she told the boy. "I'll be along shortly." She frowned at Kody. "You shouldn't be here right now. You need to leave." His brows rose, but then she nodded, and said quietly, "Yes. I have to go. I'll see you then."

Kody watched her leave, noticed how she glanced back over her shoulder, giving him a little grin with her pinked cheeks.

He wandered back to the kitchen where he spent a few moments with Maisey and her cookies, then let himself out of the school, and wondered why he'd asked the teacher to meet him. More importantly, he wondered just what he was going to say to her this evening. He had a feeling about what it was going to be, and he was already bracing himself for her rejection.

Chapter 12

Susan couldn't believe she was meeting the man, and nearly alone. What did he want to talk to her about? Luckily, the spot he'd mentioned was well in sight of several windows, and at seven in the evening, it was likely others would be wandering around. Besides, it wasn't like there was something to hide. In truth, she didn't even know what he wanted, so there was no reason to feel even a hint of shame. Or excitement.

Still, that hadn't stopped her from putting on her dark blue dress and refreshing her hair, twisting it into a low bun on her neck. Susan sighed as she checked her appearance in the small oval mirror. Plain as always.

She studied her face. Well, there wasn't much more she could do. Not unless she wanted to be accused of wearing paint on her face!

Her eyes fell on a letter from her sweetheart, and Susan sighed again. This evening's outcome might determine what she put in her next letter to him.

Quietly, Susan left her room and went outside. She saw the bench where they were to meet, and it was seven, but no one was there. Her step faltered, but she continued on. A moment later, she saw him, leaving the kitchen and hugging Maisey.

"Hello," he told Susan, coming over with that grin she'd too rapidly come to like.

"Good evening," she said, sitting on one end of the bench.

He sat on the other and nodded. "It is. Beautiful sky, good breeze, and you agreed to meet me."

Susan hesitated, then said, "Of course. You'd asked me to. But, I will admit, I have been wondering as to why."

He was quiet for a long moment. Susan couldn't tell a thing about what he was thinking. His face was perfectly still. Blank as a sheet of paper fresh from the box. Was this what was called a poker face? Him being a gambling man, it was sure he'd mastered such a thing.

Just as she went to speak, to say something, anything, to break the silence that was starting to feel uncomfortable, he spoke.

"I did. And thank you for that."

She nodded, waiting.

"I..." he stopped, and then glanced at her, looking uneasy.

The expression startled her, really. Each time she'd seen him, he was relaxed, carefree. Cocky. Except for that time in the diner, when he appeared as though he had the weight of the world upon his shoulders. Were those his true emotions? Or did he wear some sort of a mask over his true self?

"I'm not sure how to say this," he finally said. "So, I'm just going to say it. Straight out."

"That's sometimes the best way," Susan agreed, trying to ignore the strange thumping of her heart.

"I know it sounds foolish. I don't really know you. You seem to dislike me." He shot her a glance, then continued, when Susan didn't say anything. "But there's something about you. I'm not sure what it is. I just know that I can't seem to stop thinking about you. And I wondered if you maybe felt any of that."

Susan's chest felt tight, and she could hardly hear over the blood rushing to her face. "I...I do," she whispered.

"I understand we're in a challenging situation," he continued. "You're a teacher, and likely have no plans to leave that. The school needs you. The children need you. I won't make you choose. Then, there's the matter of the fact I back the school. And people might talk if they knew. Think I was forcing you into something."

"I'd deny that," Susan burst out, then, calmer now, added, "though I do appreciate your thoughtfulness."

"What about the fact I used to be a gambler?" he asked her.

That required a little more thought. But it wasn't anything Susan hadn't been thinking about. The words he'd said, spoke volumes. Used to be. He had a good reputation, otherwise. Mrs. Washington felt strongly about him, and so had the old man in front of the saloon.

Chances were, if she asked around, others would also be of a high opinion. But the thing was, none of them would be potentially courting her. He would be. And would his reputation hurt her in some way?

"You don't have to give me an answer right now," he told her. "You could think about it. For as long as you need." He looked away again, and gave a small frown. "I need to take care of some business first, though. Before we could consider courting."

"Would that business be in the form of cards and coin?" Susan asked tightly.

A concern that had been in her burst forth before she could stop it. He claimed not to be a gambler anymore, but hadn't she heard him using the very words gambling men used? *Bet. Wager.*

He looked at her, surprised. But before he could say anything, she stood. "I don't want to know. Once a gambling man, always a gambling man. It doesn't matter if I'm attracted to you. Facts are, it's hard to change, and not all people do."

She spun away, but his hand stopped her, and he rushed to the front of her. "Now wait a minute," he protested. "You've got to let me at least answer. That's how a conversation works. We both get turns at talking."

Then, he grinned, and this one lit up his whole face. "I just realized; you said you are attracted to me."

Susan's face burned, but she still met his gaze, indifferently. "Perhaps."

He brought a hand up to her cheek, and ran the backs of his fingers down it, slowly. Susan was sure she'd never felt anything like that before. Her breath hitched, and she felt frozen to the spot.

"No, cards aren't my business anymore, Sunshine. Not the gambling kind, anyway," he told her. His hand dropped, and he said, "You may not recall I mentioned how I write a woman. I'm not going to lead her on, and give her the hopes of something, when in my heart, I've fallen for you."

Susan's eyes widened at both his thoughtfulness and his honesty, for she had forgotten. Her lips parted slightly, but nothing came out of them.

"I'm not that kind of a man, to play false or loose with another's emotions," he told her. "What you see is what you get."

Then, he winked at her. "And I can tell you like what you see." His fingers brushed against hers, and his voice dropped, "I like what I see too."

Susan's pulse raced, but she managed to say, "Then I will wait. Until that's settled. It's a very noble thing of you to do."

Guilt filled her then. Here he was, thinking of the woman he'd been writing. What of her, and the man she'd been writing? How head over heels was she with this man in front of her that her sweetheart had slipped her mind whenever he was around? Yes, there was a letter she needed to write as well. But what would she say? Should she say anything? Should she wait? Be sure he was truthful?

"It's not noble," he told her, shaking his head of curls. "It's the right thing to do. And the right thing isn't always easy, and it's often at a price, but more time with you is worth it to me."

Such words had never been spoken to Susan before. In fact, she'd never thought she would ever be told such a thing. There was no insincerity in his voice, and his eyes were focused on her, blazing into her. Their fingers still touched, even though he wasn't outright holding her hand.

"Just give me a few days," he told her. "That's all I ask. Keep your heart saved for me until then? Even if it turns out we aren't suited for each other, at least we'll know. I'll know. And then I can sleep again at night, without your face haunting me."

It was so foolish, so romantic, that Susan couldn't help it. She laughed. "You have a far different opinion of me than most."

"It's because somehow, though you are the most infuriating woman I know, you are also the one I want to be with," he told her.

Then, before Susan could even blink, he'd brought her palm up to his lips, dropped a kiss onto it, and then turned, vanishing into the evening's shadows as if he'd never even been there.

Chapter 13

Kody couldn't stop pacing. He was anxious about meeting the woman he'd been writing. They were meeting at the diner. A simple place. A cup of something to drink, a bite to eat...it was the least he could do. After all, he was going to be letting the woman down. Potentially hurting her.

He wondered if she'd cry. If she did, what would he do? Kody didn't want to make her upset. But he couldn't string her along. That might be worse. The woman deserved love. Deserved to have a man devoted to her, thinking only of her. And, after meeting that teacher, he knew he wasn't the man this mail-order woman needed.

His stomach was churning like that time he'd gone out on a boat in a storm. He hoped something might settle it, and fast. Problem was, he didn't want anything inside it right now.

When he pushed open the diner, a quick glance around showed there were no single women there. There weren't even two women together—in case she'd been too worried to come alone.

Kody sat at a table, and waited, letting the waitress know he was waiting for someone. She dropped off some water, and he thanked her, then resumed nervously tapping his fingers on the table and his toes on the wooden plank floor.

A few moments later, he was surprised to see the teacher from the school come in. She glanced around, saw him and smiled, but then sat at a table by herself. More time passed. Still no woman. Kody glanced over at the teacher. She looked worried, and was biting her lip, and staring into her tea.

He wondered if something had upset her, and that's why she was there. It wouldn't hurt to go over and say hello. He could still keep an eye out for the woman he was meeting.

It was strange the woman wasn't here yet. She'd once mentioned that punctuality was important to her. Had something happened to her? He hoped not.

Kody got up and walked over to the teacher. It would be nice to have a friendly face for a few moments to talk with. "Waiting for someone?"

"Uh, yes," she said, a hint of nervousness in her voice as she set down her tea.

"Me too," he said, and shook his head. "Guess she's not coming."

He turned back to go to his table, when a small hand landed on his arm. "Wait. She?" the teacher asked. He was surprised to see she'd stood up.

Kody hesitated. There was a strange look on her face that he didn't quite understand. "Yes. The...the woman I'd been writing. I asked her to meet me here. I think I told you that? To tell her I can't. That..."

His words trailed off as he observed her face. First, it had paled, then it had turned a strange red, now, it was a decidedly green. What would it do next?

"You okay?" he asked her, squinting.

"I...I'm not sure," she said, sitting heavily in her chair. "You see, I was to meet the man I'd been writing."

Now, it was Kody's turn to sit, near falling into the chair that was thankfully nearby. He swallowed hard. His mouth felt dry. "You don't think..."

She sat, looking at him. Her eyes were wide, and her face was pale again. She stared at him, and Kody wondered if that was shock. If it was, what did his face look like? He was feeling mighty shocked himself.

This wasn't something he'd bet on. No way. He'd have lost the hand, if someone had bet him this would happen. If what he was thinking happened, did.

He forced a breath in his tight chest. "Are you...are you..." His words were stuck. Kody signaled for the waitress to bring him a drink. When she'd left him water, he drank half of it, before asking, "Are you Susan Louden?"

When she didn't answer, he reached into his pocket and pulled out a letter. She gasped, and dug into her handbag, pulling out a letter of her own.

For a long moment, neither said anything, just stared at the other. Time felt like it had stopped. Frozen them and everything else in place. Just as quickly, they were jerked back into the moment. Then, they both laughed. It was so loud, Kody was sure that everyone was staring at them, but he didn't care.

"I'll be," he said, sitting back in his chair, a grin on his face and tears from laughing so hard in his eyes. "I can't believe it. It was you I was writing all this time, Sunshine."

"I never knew you were Mr. Hall," Susan told him.

"Kody," he told her. "Please."

She laughed softly and shook her head. "I can't believe it. Do you know, this might have all come to light sooner had I known your name one of the times I'd seen you at the school. Why, as many times as we'd met, I'd never learned it."

Kody blinked a few times. "You're right," he said slowly in surprise. "And I never knew yours. I always forgot to ask it. And then, it didn't seem important."

"Why not?" Susan asked him.

"Because we were too busy talking," he answered.

She nodded. "I understand."

"What do you think you'd have done, if you had learned it was me?" he asked curiously. "I mean, you gave me a piece of your mind a time or two."

Susan blushed. "Because I didn't know who you were. I was concerned about the children," she explained.

"I know," he told her. He frowned. "You might have thought I was spying on you. Up to no good. It's likely better this way."

"You might just be right," she told him, with a small frown of her own. "That's just how I'd think."

They were quiet for a moment, then she asked, "What now?"

"Now? Well, my appetite has returned. Do you want to have dinner still? And, well, I guess I don't have to tell you that it's not going to work between us, because I met a woman I'm interested in."

Susan teased him, "I guess not." She glanced down, and said, "Hopefully I don't ever hear that from you. I...I really was interested in the man I'd been writing to. Then, the other night, when we were talking...I felt torn."

Kody didn't know what to do. He couldn't stop grinning. Things were feeling hopeful. Moving in the right direction. "There's something we do need to do," he told her.

"What's that?" Susan asked.

They were interrupted by the waitress, wanting to take their orders. Once she'd walked away, Kody held out his hand. When Susan looked at it, not understanding, he said, "Kody Hall, ma'am. A real pleasure to meet you."

"Susan Louden," she answered, with a smile that filled her face. "Thank you for inviting me to dinner."

Chapter 14

As they sat over their meals, dumplings smothered in a thick white gravy, green beans, boiled carrots, and fluffy biscuits and butter, Susan had to admit that she was enjoying herself.

Once she'd gotten over the surprise that the sweetheart she'd been writing—and had planned to potentially give up—was none other than the man she kept running into, she was more than amused. She felt right. Even if that felt like such an odd thing to admit.

"I really am sorry I startled you, and made you worried those first two times we met," Kody said. "It was never my intention to make anyone think that I was doing something inappropriate at the school. I just wanted to check on the children. See for myself they were doing well."

"I overreacted a little," Susan admitted. "Though I'm grateful you understand that their protection was in the forefront of my mind." She bit her lip. "Even if I keep making little mistakes."

"I do. But, mistakes? In what way?" Kody asked.

Susan shook her head, as she slid her fork into a dumpling. "I forget sometimes, and call the school an orphanage. Mrs. Washington says that could bring up bad memories for the children. I'm trying very hard not to think of it as such. That's really the last thing I want to do. Then, there was that time I raised my voice, angry at you, and frightened Josh. I know we aren't supposed to do that either."

Slowly, Kody nodded, and took a bite. When he'd swallowed, he said, "Everybody makes mistakes sometimes. Go easier on yourself. You're still new. Learning. The kids will understand. Betty does too."

"Thank...thank you," she said softly. "I appreciate that. It really isn't my intention to make any of the children upset."

"I know that. Now, tell me," Kody said. "Do you enjoy being there?"

"I do," Susan said. She shook her head again, but this time it was in wonder, not shame over her actions. "Everything is so well thought out. The children all, generally, seem so happy. I love how Mrs. Washington cares for them so deeply. It makes me want to be a better person for them."

"I understand." Kody sighed. "It does me too. That's why I've tried to change."

Susan stilled, then asked, almost nervously, "Is...is it as hard as it seems it might be?" At his puzzled look, she continued, "My grandfather tried many times to change his ways. He never could. There was always something that pulled him back into what he was trying to give up. It eventually ruined him. Hurt our family."

"I see. So, that's made you a little wary about others? And their ability to change?" Kody asked.

She nodded.

The waitress refilled their drinks, and once she'd left, Kody answered.

"For me, gambling is a part of who I am. It doesn't matter what it is. Will it or won't it. It's part of the fun of the guessing. Of pushing myself to do more. Study people better. Observe things closer. But as for gambling with cards," Kody locked eyes with her, "Gambling for money, I'm done with that. It was a short time. Done simply because I was curious. And I stopped. But if you'd ask me not to place a wager on whether Meggie over there is going to have a girl or a boy..." He grinned, nodding toward the waitress. "That's a little harder. Especially when I know most all the women in town have their opinions."

Susan laughed. "Yes, they do. And, for that, I see your point. An educated guess or a bit of an old wives tale might not be any different from a wager or a gamble." She bit her lip. "There's no prize to be won, just the bragging rights, I suppose. So, that's fine by me. That sort of gamble."

"Then, you'd be okay if I said I knew I was taking a gamble on getting to know you, and hoping you liked me half as much as I liked you?"

Kody's eyes pierced through her, and Susan's heart started to flutter. Her stomach swirled, but not in a bad way. It was warm. Tingly. Excited.

"I—"

"Miss Louden! Oh! Kody! Thank goodness. I don't have to find you too."

They both looked over, and half rose. Mrs. Washington stood before them, her hair, usually neatly bound at the neck, with loose strands, and her face red from exertion.

"What's wrong?" Kody asked, his voice tense. He stopped next to her.

"Josh. He's missing. We've searched everywhere." Mrs. Washington's voice rose in panic. "You know it rained last night. A terrible storm. If he fell into the water..."

Kody threw money on the table, grabbed Mrs. Washington's shoulders, and said, "I will find him. Don't you worry."

He looked at Susan. "I'm sorry to cut this short."

"I'll help you search," Susan said, fear rising in her as she grabbed her handbag. Where could the child be? He'd seemed so happy.

"Check around the school again, top to bottom," Kody ordered. "If the other children don't know he's missing, tell them. Everyone search. They may know a place a child hides an adult doesn't."

He glanced at Mrs. Washington. "Any idea why he left? That may give me a clue on where to find him."

Her lips thinned as she pressed them together in thought. "No, I don't think so. As I made my rounds, it seemed as though all was well. He was playing with the others, and nothing seemed amiss.'"

"Something had to have upset him, though," Kody mused. His brow was furrowed. "The boy wouldn't go unless something had."

"Actually..." The headmistress nodded slowly. "Some of the other children were playing a game that was unusually noisy. Miss Ashe asked them to quiet just a little, and I remember now." She shook her head as she looked up at Kody, "He said the oddest thing."

"What's that?" Kody asked her.

Susan bit her lip, glancing between the two. Both were so focused. So sure of what they were doing. She wished she knew what to do. Where the boy might go. If only she'd made more of an effort to get to know him. To get to know all of them. It was clear, suddenly, that she wasn't just hired to be a teacher. She was hired to also be a caregiver. And part of that duty was to care for each child in whatever way they needed. Friendship being paramount, especially to these children without parents to talk to.

"He said, 'Sometimes there isn't a whole lot of quiet here, and I don't want to get anybody in trouble.'" Mrs. Washington wrung her hands. "Does that mean anything to you?"

Susan glanced at Kody. He was nodding slowly. "Perhaps."

He rushed to the diner's door, and glanced backward once more. "We'll find him. Just keep looking. I'll start my search at the creek. Let the sheriff know. Send someone after me if you find him there at the school. But not a child. Not with the water so strong."

The sky darkened just then, and fat drops of rain fell. The last thing Susan saw was the grim expression on Kody's face as he raced down the street.

Chapter 15

The sky above him was dark, making it appear as though it was far later than it was. Regardless, Kody knew there wasn't going to be too much daylight left. He had to find the boy. Especially if he was where he thought he might be.

He shot a last look over his shoulder as he left Susan and Mrs. Washington behind. They were hurrying away, in opposite directions, and he could hear them calling for the boy.

Though Kody had long legs, and usually didn't get winded, the combination of both fear and concern for Josh's welfare made his chest tight, and he struggled to draw in deep enough breaths as he hurried through the town.

A breeze picked up, sending leaves that weren't yet wet swirling. Kody coughed as dust kicked up, and hoped they weren't in for a twister. It had been a while, but the way the wind was moving...was it possible?

Kody turned down one of the alleyways, a spot he was almost too large to squeeze between. The town had tried not to build too many buildings touching another, knowing that if one caught fire, those on the other side would be sure to burn down as well. While some folks didn't care, choosing to do the usual town layout of buildings touching, a few, like the dressmaker and the shoemaker, had about a two-foot gap between their buildings. Just enough for him to slip through to take as a shortcut to the creek.

After maybe five minutes of running, Kody spotted the creek ahead and slowed. The water was rushing, and the heavy rain that had started only added to the water.

"God, we need a miracle," Kody muttered as he pushed his wet hair from his eyes. "This doesn't look good."

In his heart, he knew he'd find Josh nearby. He just hoped he'd find the boy alive.

The skies flashed, a loud crack of thunder rang out, and the hairs on the back of Kody's neck stood up, but the rain stopped, and he looked upward in gratitude. "Thank you."

He scanned the area. This wasn't quite the fishing spot, but it was a good place to start.

"Josh!" he called loudly. "Josh!"

Kody worked his way along the bank, looking for anything—anyone—flowing down in the water. The creek fed into a river, about fifteen miles away. He just hoped he was in time. If he wasn't—

"I won't think like that," Kody said firmly. "Josh! Where are you?"

Usually, alongside the creek was a peaceful place. There were large trees for shade, a grassy bank, and rocks aplenty for a body to sit on and soak their feet in the cool water, or to cross from one side to the next.

Unless it stormed. Then, at times, the water would overflow the creek, and turn the beautiful spot into something still beautiful, in a wild way, but also incredibly dangerous.

Kody approached the spot where the schoolchildren usually went. Right now, it was vastly different from how it had looked a few days ago, when blankets spread out were filled with families and children. Now, the grass was near flattened from the rain, and muddy patches sucked at his boots.

"Josh! Josh!"

His voice was getting hoarse, and Kody absently rubbed at his throat. It was starting to hurt from shouting so loudly. Could the boy even hear him over the rushing water? He had to hope so, or else the despair he was feeling might take over.

There was no choice. He had to find the boy if he was here. And Kody was willing to bet his all that he was. That same feeling he had that he'd never been able to explain to others washed over him. That *feeling* that he was close to the win.

From the corner of his eye, Kody caught sight of something large rushing down the creek. He felt sick to his stomach as his head snapped around, before he realized it was simply a large branch, not a boy.

"Josh! No one's mad at you!" he shouted. "But I'm real worried. I want to make sure you are okay."

He continued up the creek. There were some bushes ahead, about a half mile. Maybe he'd sought shelter there.

Kody moved that way as fast as he could, his boots sliding in muddy patches. Twice, he thought he heard something and spun around, but there was no one out there but himself.

A turn scrap of fabric caught his eye, and Kody grabbed it, inspecting it. Could it have come from the boy? He wasn't sure. It could have been anyone's. He didn't even know what Josh was wearing.

There was another flash of lightning, and another shock of thunder, but the rain held. The sky was darker now, and Kody knew that within the hour, he wouldn't be able to see his hand in front of his face. He had to find the boy. Had to find him soon.

As Kody finally approached the bushes, he thought he saw one shake. "Josh!" he yelled, heading toward it, but instead of the boy, a scared rabbit hopped away.

Frustration filled his every pore, until the wind picked up, and another boom of thunder washed the emotion into fear. The worst thing imaginable had happened. A boy he was responsible for was gone. Likely hurt or dead. He'd let him down, just like he'd sworn to himself never to do.

Chapter 16

Worry filled every inch of Susan. She was anxious about Josh. Why had the boy left? Would Kody find him? Maybe he was back at the school, hiding somewhere none of them knew about. Or maybe he was lost. Hurt. Kidnapped.

She shuddered. She should have been more attentive. The boy was in her care as well. It seemed her preoccupation with Kody had distracted her at a time when she was needed most—and had let the child down.

As she and Mrs. Washington left the diner and headed toward the sheriff's office, her thoughts flitted from Kody to Josh to Kody again.

He said he wasn't gambling for money. However, despite what she'd told Kody, about agreeing that guessing—or gambling—on what gender a newborn baby would be, Susan was feeling uneasy. Could a woman dedicate her life to children while being associated with a gambler? Even if their relationship right now was simply seeing where it was going.

Josh missing was proof that she shouldn't let herself be distracted away from the children. What if she'd neglected a sign? Didn't notice Josh was trying to tell her something. Needed her help.

Constant worry filled her, and a glance at Mrs. Washington showed the older woman was beyond frantic.

"We will find him," Susan tried to assure her, even though she was worried it wasn't the truth.

The headmistress's shoulders sagged. "This is all my fault. I'm entrusted with these children. I've let them down," she said, her voice catching.

Susan didn't have a chance to answer, as they came to the sheriff's office and Mrs. Washington burst in. "We've a student missing," she said, commanding the room.

Once the sheriff and his deputy left to join in the search, Mrs. Washington started back toward the school. "We will search every nook," she told Susan, resolve in her voice, "every cranny. There is to be no rest until the child is found."

"Yes, ma'am," Susan said as she hurried alongside of her.

They reached the school quickly, and Mrs. Washington went from teacher to teacher, telling them to search again.

Susan searched the third floor with her students. They went from room to room, carefully searching.

Now and again, Susan glanced through a window, grateful to see that though it was growing dark, the sky held. Rain would simply make the matter worse.

"Will we find him?" one of the younger children asked her.

"We will," Susan promised firmly. "There are several men right now outside searching for him."

"But he'll miss dinner," another child said. "He'll be hungry."

"Mrs. Washington won't let that happen," another said confidently. "She takes good care of us."

Susan's thoughts drowned out their small voices as she continued to search, peering in each cabinet, wardrobe, and under each bed.

Yes, the older woman did take good care of them. And she had also done the same for Kody.

Kody. He said he wanted to change. Had changed. But could a person? What if something happened that drove them back to the object of their addiction? In her grandfather's case, it was drinking.

She flinched, hearing her grandfather's raspy voice as he told her grandmother, "You drove me to it."

Susan and the children moved to another room.

"Maybe this time, Miss Louden will let him stay," a little girl said, sniffling.

Her feet froze to the ground, and Susan turned to the girl. "What did you say?"

"I-I-I didn't mean for you to overhear me," the child whispered.

"I am not angry," Susan assured her, plastering on what she hoped was a friendly smile. "But if you know something that may help us find Josh, I need to hear it."

"He-he told us you told Mr. Kody he couldn't be here," the little girl said. "It upset Josh something awful. All of us too." She looked up, and tears collected at the corners of her eyes. "Mr. Kody's our friend. We don't want him going away. Please, Miss Louden. Don't make him leave."

Susan frowned, and her brows drew together as she tried to remember when she'd said such a thing. Then, it came to her. When Kody had asked to meet her. Josh had been nearby, and she'd sent him outside. The child must have misunderstood.

But had he run away because of that? Susan closed her eyes. Had...had she driven him to do that? Much as her grandfather accused her grandmother of driving him to drink? What if she ended up doing the same to Kody?

She'd been harsh the first few times they met, though with good reason. She'd never let herself think otherwise. But...what if she continued to be that way? What if *she* couldn't change? She'd been so focused, so worried about him, she'd neglected the fact that she had her own things to overcome. Her sharp words being one of them.

Susan sank down, her back against the wall, and dropped her face into her hands.

"We'll get 'im back, Miss Louden," a little boy said solemnly. "This is all our home now. We're his family, and we're not gonna stop lookin' till we find 'im."

His words, spoken so innocently, so filled with trust, bolstered her. Susan smiled at the children and then rose. "Right you are. And once we find him, we will make sure that Josh knows how important he is to all of us. Mr. Kody too."

As the children nodded, everyone resumed their search again.

Susan felt determination fill her. And a realization. This was one of those things in life you just had to have faith in the outcome. Trust that everything would work out the way that it should. The same with her relationship with Kody, and his penchant for gambling.

What was needed right now wasn't doubt, or fear, or worry. No second guessing, no borrowing trouble where there was none.

No.

Susan would be strong. Confident. Have the faith of these children. And if she was lacking, which sometimes she was, she'd borrow some of theirs until she found her own.

The thing to do right now, was to find Josh. Nothing else mattered. The rest would all work out, she was sure.

Her future, her relationship with Kody, her apprehension about his habits, and even her own shortcomings. It would all work out. She would have—did have—faith.

"Does Mr. Kody know?" a child asked. "Maybe he can help us."

Susan nodded. "Mr. Kody is looking for him right now."

"Then he'll find him," a girl said, grinning widely and showing a missing tooth. "I know it."

"I do too," Susan said, smiling at the children, as she led them to the next room.

And, somehow, she did. But a wave of goosebumps washed over her as thunder shook the house, and she hoped that he'd find the boy unharmed. That was the part she wasn't sure on.

Chapter 17

"Josh? Where are you?" Kody called again, ignoring the ache in his throat. There were only whispers of light left. He wouldn't give up, no, but he would need to get a lantern in order to continue the search.

No matter that the storm had that feel about it that it would return, Kody wouldn't leave a stone unturned until he found the child. It wasn't just the raging water that could knock a grown man off his feet, strike his head on a rock, and carry his unconscious body to a larger body of water.

It was the wild animals that would come out with the moon, eager for easy prey.

"Josh," Kody called. "I'm not leaving without you. But I will have to get a lantern soon. You can save me the walking, if you just show up right now."

He waited a moment, hoping his appeal would work, then slumped his shoulders. Nothing. Not a sound, not a rustle of the bushes, nothing.

"I'll be back," he called again. "I'm not going to stop until I make sure you're all right. We're family, Josh. I'm not leaving you behind."

Kody set off, his legs taking each stride in full strength as he hurried back to town. He needed a lantern. Maybe ought to get a blanket too. Some food? He could shove a few things in his pocket, both for himself if he had to search all night, and the boy, when he found him.

There was no doubt in his mind that he would. Only a matter of when. It felt like an invisible clock was counting down, and as the cry of a coyote made his neck prickle, Kody decided he'd better grab a rifle too. Rifle, lantern, food. That was the most important. He couldn't carry the blanket as well.

"Mr. Kody?"

Kody's heart nearly stopped, then he turned, seeing a figure in the dim light. Josh! He was safe.

Rushing over to him, Kody grabbed the boy's shoulders and pulled him into a hug, then frantically looked him over. "Are you all right? Are you hurt anywhere?"

"No, sir," Josh said, his voice a little muffled as Kody pulled him closer for another crushing hug.

"Why'd you run away?" Kody asked. "Everyone was so worried. I was so worried."

Even with very little light, Kody could see the hesitation on the boy's face. "Do I have to tell you, Mr. Kody?"

"Well," Kody said, running a hand through his hair, "I guess not. But if there's a problem, I can't help get it fixed if I don't know what it is."

When Josh didn't answer, Kody said, "Let's start walking back toward the school. Mrs. Washington will be in a real mess. The sooner she sees you, the better. I bet you want some dinner too."

"Yes, sir," Josh said.

As they walked along, the rushing water filled Kody's ears, but not much else. Finally, Josh said, "The problem is me."

"You? How so?" Kody asked, his eyebrows raised. He couldn't imagine why the boy would think so.

"I heard Miss Louden tell you that you weren't supposed to be there. I know she got real mad one of the other times you were talking to me. And, well," Josh stopped talking, and Kody could have sworn he heard a sniffle, but he couldn't see. It was so dark now, he was walking toward the small light ahead that he hoped was the school.

"Well, if I weren't there, you couldn't get in trouble. The other kids need you. The school needs you. I know it's your school," Josh told him.

"How do you know that?" Kody asked.

"I just do. I seem to always know the things about things." Josh shrugged.

Kody saw the slight movement and froze. When Josh paused his walking, Kody caught up. "You mean, like which frog will jump the higher? Which stick will float better on the water under the bridge?"

"That's right," Josh said. "All that and more. Even who is telling truths or not. I do it from watching. Listening. Instincts, I guess."

"Well, I'll be," Kody muttered. A slow grin came over his face. "You're just like me."

"I'd be proud to be just like you," Josh told him. "But I reckon I've a ways to go. Sometimes it gets real noisy. Makes me feel jumpy, and I just got to get away. I don't see anybody else doing that. Especially you."

Kody wrapped an arm around the boy's shoulders. They were still thin from not eating enough, but he felt sure in a few months, the boy would be sturdier and fill out. And he was going to be around to see it, and everything else this kid did. He hoped.

"Others feel that way too. They just don't show it," Kody assured him. He shot Josh a grin. "I'm not going anywhere. And I'm going to help you get wherever you want to go."

"You mean it?" Josh's voice wobbled.

"Sure as the sun will rise in the morning," Kody promised.

The school rose up ahead, but Kody slowed. Josh did too.

"You know why I started this place?" Kody asked.

"I reckon to help us kids who needed somebody," Josh said.

"That's right," Kody agreed. "But it's more than just helping. I don't want any of you to feel alone. We're a family here. Best of all, we're a family we got to pick."

"I don't understand," Josh said.

"It's like this," Kody told him. "I didn't get to pick my ma nor my pa. Can tell you for a fact I wouldn't have chosen either of them. But Mrs. Washington...when she offered to be my ma, I said yes. You see that? I picked her. Just like you picked coming here. You were given a choice, weren't you?"

"Yes, sir," Josh said. "And told I could leave whenever I wanted."

"That's right," Kody said. "But that didn't mean sneaking away. That meant leaving with clothes and food and a few dollars, if that was the path you thought you should take."

"Oh."

"Here, at this school, my school, you're my kid. The minute you said yes to coming here, I was going to take care of you."

The front door to the school opened, and the silhouette of Mrs. Washington filled it. A few blinks later, smaller figures came rushing out of the door toward them.

"Now, you can go if you want," Kody said, "but it's going to be when your family can give you a proper goodbye, and the promise you can come back."

He watched as Josh stared at the other children, calling to him and waving excitedly. "Or, you can stay. Decision is yours, but I know I'd love to have you around."

"You mean it?" Josh said quietly.

"You can bet on it," Kody told him.

"I bet on a lot of things," Josh said, as Kody wrapped his arm around his shoulders and they walked toward the school.

"You can bet on anything you want," Kody told him. "But best not bet on cards, or anything for money. Miss Louden doesn't like that."

They both laughed, and the next thing they knew, were surrounded by children, and teachers, and Mrs. Washington, who had grabbed Josh up as though he were no more than a baby, was crying as she held him tightly.

Kody stepped back, swallowing the lump in his throat as he watched. His eyes felt a little damp, but he figured that was all right. Wasn't every day you found a kid as sharp as a tack and just like you to be part of your family.

Getting Josh away from the abusive man who'd bought him after his parents died had been difficult, and expensive. But it was a gamble Kody knew they had to take. He'd been right.

Always was. Maybe, just maybe...Josh might be the one to take over for him one day. A little soon to tell, but—

"Kody?"

His eyes fell on Susan, who stood before him. "I'm so glad you found him," she said, wrapping her arms around herself.

"Me too. Was about to get a lantern, it had gotten so dark."

"Everyone inside," Mrs. Washington called out. "Milk and cookies for all. We've a celebration tonight! Josh has been found!"

There were cheers from the children, and Kody had hardly taken two breaths when he realized that he and Susan were alone.

"I know it isn't the best of times," she said, "but I was hoping we could finish our earlier conversation."

A feeling Kody didn't like settled into his stomach. He nodded. "Of course. Shall we go into the library?"

Chapter 18

Susan led the way to the library. Her heart was filled with relief that Josh was back. The warm welcome the others had given him had made her tear up. She only hoped the boy knew how much they all wanted him there.

Tomorrow, in her class, she'd make sure to tell him so, and afterward encourage him to come to her if he ever needed anything.

She couldn't fight the small smile at the memory of when she'd first seen him tonight. Kody's arm was slung around the boy's shoulder, and Josh had been looking at him with so much admiration in his face, while Kody had such fondness on his. If she'd had any doubt about his genuine affection for the children, it was gone.

"Let me get the door," Kody said, reaching past her. He turned the handle, and the room opened before them.

Susan walked inside, but paused, turning to see Kody looking around the room slowly, a satisfied expression on his face.

"I do love this room," he said, walking in and letting his fingers trail over the books.

"Do you enjoy reading?" Susan asked. "It's a wonderful library you've provided."

His ears pinked, and he ducked his head for a moment. "I do. All my favorites are on the shelves, though I've not chosen everything in here. I trust the judgment of you teachers."

Susan took a seat on one of the reading sofas. "I am so grateful you found Josh."

"I am too," Kody said. "I was getting a little scared, truth be told."

Susan ran her hands down her dress, and then again. She was feeling nervous. Kody sat next to her. She turned, and said, "About earlier. What you'd said."

Kody crinkled his brow. "Which part? A lot was said."

"About how you wondered...about us." Susan bit her lip, worried what he might say.

"That's right." Kody studied her. "I'd like to give us a chance. Would you?"

"Yes." Susan drew in a deep breath. "I would."

"Even though I'm a gambler at heart?" he asked her.

"I think," Susan said slowly, "you've proved me wrong. Showed me that a man can change. And even perhaps that sometimes, having those gambling instincts pays off, when used in the right way."

"How so?" Kody asked her.

"Well, how you found Josh. Also, how you are willing to take a chance on me, even though I wasn't the nicest at first."

"The kid's a lot like me," Kody said, rubbing a hand over his jaw. "I feel a huge weight of responsibility. I'm not going to let him down, and I'm not going to let you down. I'm going to be the best that I can be for you, for Josh, for the town."

"Promise me something?" Susan asked.

"You bet, Sunshine," Kody said, then grinned.

She laughed, not minding the nickname, then became serious. "Be the best that you can be for yourself too. You deserve it."

A dozen emotions flickered through Kody's face, and he swallowed hard. "Thank you," he said, his voice low. "That's about the kindest thing anyone's ever said."

"I meant it," Susan said, reaching over and resting her hand on his.

Kody smiled, and captured her hand into his, squeezing it gently.

"There is one thing," Susan said quietly.

He looked at her, concern flickering on his face.

Susan took a deep breath and continued. "Sometimes, I'm too harsh on people. I'm trying to get better. I am. I don't always think before I say things. That's not proper for a teacher, or a friend, or a sweetheart. I'm judgmental. And, well, I've been doing that to others my whole life, without even noticing my own flaws."

She lowered her head in shame. "It's wrong for me to expect others to change, and not even consider it myself."

His hand squeezed hers again. "I wouldn't want you to change," Kody said.

Susan looked up at him. "Why not?" she whispered. "Those are all horrid things."

He shrugged. "Maybe. But they serve a purpose. You left out some of the good things that come from that. Protectiveness, situational awareness, truthfulness. Anyway, if you change, you aren't the woman I fell in love with. I don't want someone else. I want you. Just as you are. If you change as time passes, like we all do, then that's fine. But don't change for me. Change because you want to."

"I...I don't know what to say," Susan whispered.

"Don't have to say anything," Kody told her.

They sat in silence for a long moment. Susan wasn't sure she'd ever felt so happy or content. It had been a long day, full of surprises and shocks, and fears, but somehow, it had ended perfectly. Even with...

"You know, you've actually done me a favor," Susan said suddenly.

"How so?" he asked.

"I wasn't quite sure how I felt about that man I was writing. Then, when I knew you were interested in me, I was worried that I'd have to choose between you. You've solved that problem for me nicely. Thank you."

Kody laughed. It was a full belly laugh. "I'm happy to be of service," he told her.

"I am sorry, though," Susan said, searching his face. "For the past. For the times I wasn't kind."

"I understand why you did it," Kody said, taking her other hand into his. He raised her hands and pressed a kiss in each palm.

"I figure it's worked out anyway. I admit, I fell a little in love with the woman writing me letters. But every time I got one, I was half scared to open it, fearing she'd find out I was a gambling man. She was so proper. So perfect. Almost felt untouchable, and I sure didn't feel good enough. But when we met... I fell for you pretty fast. Might have been that spitfire in you." Kody smiled at her. "I like a woman who isn't afraid to speak her mind."

Susan just shook her head, and stared at their joined hands. "Are we crazy?" she asked, hoping he would say no.

"Sure are," he told her.

Her eyes flew to his.

Kody kept talking. "But crazy isn't always bad. Matter of fact, I'm crazy about you. I'm glad you're willing to see where we go."

"I am too," Susan said. "But one thing I need to make clear."

"I'm listening," Kody said.

"As I'd said in my letters, I love teaching. I especially enjoy working with these children. I'm not wanting to leave here, yet. Will that...will that change your mind about our relationship, in the future?"

Kody glanced off into the distance, then studied her for a moment. "You do realize this place is mine, don't you? Whatever woman I marry will need to be involved with it deeply. Need to love and care for the children. If that's you, and you want to teach still, I won't stop you. If that's you, in some other capacity here at the school, I won't stop you there either. But me and the school and the kids, we're a package deal. We go together, or not at all."

Susan felt so light, it was hard to believe she wasn't floating. She threw herself at him, her arms wrapped around his neck tightly. "Kody Hall, I don't think I could love you more if I tried," she whispered into his ear.

"I'll take that bet," Kody teased.

Susan laughed, and pulled back, smacking at his shoulder. "I'll *bet* you would," she said. "But remember, you're an example to the others."

"Kody? Are you still here, dear?" Mrs. Washington called from the hallway.

Kody rose and winked at Susan. "Spoilsport," he said, heading toward the library door.

Chapter 19

Kody stood in front of the general store, and heavily set a box in the back of the wagon. As he paused to wipe at his brow, the sound of laughter trickled out from the nearby saloon.

"Full house!" someone shouted from within, and Kody could imagine the grins and groans. If he sniffed, he was sure he would be able to smell tobacco and sour drinks, sweat and perfume.

He closed his eyes and breathed in deeply. His ears picked up every sound. His fingers tingled, and a familiar itch dug its way through his shoulders.

"Makes you miss it, don't it?" Carl asked, from where he'd been sitting in a rocking chair.

"A little bit," Kody admitted, opening his eyes. He gave a crooked grin. "But I've got something better now, and not willing to gamble it away."

"That's a smart man," Carl said with a nod. He pointed to Josh. "You listen to him, now. Kody's a real smart 'un."

Josh grinned up at him. "I know it. And I also know, we can't bet on cards, or Miss Louden will get mad."

Kody laughed, and grabbed the next box from Josh. They were taking supplies back to the school. He'd be hiring a man to help do this work. The way his back was twinging was reminding him he was getting a little old for it.

"You know, Josh," Kody said, leading Josh over to the bakery, where they bought a lemonade and a cookie each, "we all make mistakes in life. Matter of fact, we probably all make them each day. But a real man, like you and me and Carl," he handed Carl a lemonade and a cookie as he sat next to him on one of the rocking chairs, "a real man tries hard not to make them again."

"But what happens if he does?" Josh asked, sitting next to Kody. He looked between Kody and Carl, who was nodding along.

"Well, then he atones for the mistake. That means, he tries to fix whatever he did. If it was a lie, he apologizes. If he broke something, he fixes it." Kody took a long drink and leaned back with a sigh, resting his head against the store's front.

"And if he was too slow to hire a man to run Mrs. Washington's and the school's errands, he finds one." Kody looked over. "Carl, want a job? It's fixing stuff, picking up supplies, helping keep an eye on the school. I need a man I can trust."

Carl sat up so quick, his hat fell over one eye. He pushed it back up and asked, "You mean it?"

"Couldn't ask for a better man," Kody said, dusting his hands off from crumbs. "I've just been putting off stopping out your way to ask because I've been busy. See what it gets me?" He jerked a thumb toward the wagon. "I ought to be in my study, checking on my businesses. Don't worry about the heavy lifting. We got a few older boys at the school who do the unloading, and James and Grace said they'd load for you."

"I'd like nothing better," Carl said, grinning so wide Kody saw his missing tooth. "The missus be right pleased to hear. A respectable job." He stood.

"Speaking of the missus," Kody said. "If she ever wants to get out of the house a little, Maisey, our cook, sure could use a hand. Tell her to join you one day. See what Maisey needs, and if she's interested."

Carl's jaw bobbed for a moment, before he answered, his eyes full of tears, "I'll tell her now. You're one in a million, Kody."

There was no need to answer. Kody watched as Carl hurried off, a spring in his step he hadn't seen in a long time. Carl and his wife would be a blessing for the school. It would benefit them too, financially, as it was hard for an older couple to make a living. They'd never had children of their own, but were as nurturing as they came, and Kody bet they'd fit in just fine there.

"Mr. Kody," Josh asked. "Anything else I need to load up?"

"Just yourself," Kody said, and slapped his knee. "Hate to do it, but best we get on back. I'm sure glad you rode out with me today."

"I'm glad too." Josh grinned. "I like being with you."

They climbed in the wagon, and Kody glanced over to see Josh squinting at two birds that had landed on a hitching post. "Which do you think flies off first?" Kody asked as he studied the pair.

"Left one," Josh answered, without hesitation.

"Me too," Kody said.

They sat watching until the birds took flight. It was the left who went first. Kody and Josh grinned at each other in the kind of satisfaction only another kindred spirit could understand.

"Let's go," Kody said, and shook the reins.

The drive back wasn't too long, and as they neared the school, he saw Susan sitting outside, a book in her lap on the bench where she'd yelled at him at all that time ago. She raised a hand in a wave, and Josh nudged him.

"Mr. Kody, are you two going to get married one day?"

Kody touched his chest pocket and said, "We'll find out this afternoon. I'm going to ask her."

Chapter 20

Susan walked into her classroom, and was surprised to see the children gathered around Kody with wide grins on their faces. They were whispering back and forth excitedly, but she couldn't hear what about.

"What are you up to?" she asked, crossing her arms over her chest.

"Just saying hello to my children, and now leaving so you can teach your class," Kody said, eyes wide in mock innocence.

Susan tried not to roll her eyes, or let her lips twitch up into a smile. Whatever he was up to, she was sure she'd find out soon. For now, it was time for reading.

It was a lovely day. Cloudless, a light breeze that floated fragrant honeysuckle on it, with just a slight whiff of the hay that had been brought in that morning for the six older horses Kody had bought the students.

It seemed the school expanded, in some new way, every few months, and it always amazed Susan how he was able to do such a thing and yet, how much it also benefited each of the students.

"Please take out your readers. Read the story to yourself that is on pages twenty-four through thirty, and then we will read aloud," Susan said, walking slowly up and down the rows of desks.

The books were pulled out, and she didn't miss the small giggles or traded looks. Susan tried not to let it irritate her, but it was most unlike her students. She would have to talk to Kody about coming into her classroom and riling up her class. He knew better.

"Settle," she ordered sternly, and walked to the front of her desk to grade papers while the children read.

For the next while, the classroom was quiet, except for the sound of paper turning in the books, the scratching of her pen, feet shuffling, and the sparrow who had decided to serenade them on a branch outside the window.

It was the last class of the day, and Susan would admit that she was also feeling restless. The urge for fresh air had been so great, she'd spent her lunch outdoors reading, with an apple and some cheese.

Susan's mind wandered as she looked through the window at the sparrow. Why had Kody been in here?

Sometimes, she would come to her classroom and find a small bunch of flowers from him, or a sweet, or a note. But she'd never spotted him in there talking to the students before she arrived. Just passed him in the hallway, or seen him leaving. Today was different. Felt different.

Her gaze lingered on each student. Her classroom had grown in size slightly. There was always room for one more, was Mrs. Washington's motto, and indeed, the school could hold a good number more, as it had been built with a large number of students in mind. She, herself, had an additional three children from when she'd started.

Children. Susan had always thought of them as children or students, but since Josh's disappearance, something in her had changed. Each one of them, even those she didn't know well yet, became her children. Susan would have thought it strange, except for the fact she knew the other teachers felt the same.

There, they really were a family, and it felt good to be surrounded by them, and knowing that she was helping to raise and provide for them.

Some of the older boys would be leaving the classrooms soon. Two wanted to stay on at the school, one caring for the horses, the other doing handyman jobs with Carl.

The old man had been a most unexpected employee at the school, but he and his wife fit right in, and were loved by all.

Susan smiled, and shook her head. What an unlikely lot they were all here. All brought together by Kody, who just seemed to know how they'd all fit in and work together, imperfectness and all.

As one by one, the students finished reading and sat patiently, hands folded on their books, Susan smiled. "Well done. I hope you enjoyed that story. Shall we read together now? Let us play close attention to pronouncing some of the large words in the story."

She picked up her book, opened to the correct page, and stood before the class. "We will start by rows. One paragraph each, please."

The children looked at each other with an expression Susan couldn't decipher. She tried to keep herself from getting upset. What were they up to? Something, she could sense it, but what?

"I'm waiting," Susan said, raising a brow.

"Yes, Miss Louden," all of the children said.

The child at the first desk took a deep breath at the others and nodded. As one, the children said, "Miss Louden, will you marry Mr. Kody?"

Susan's jaw dropped. "Wh-wha—" she was sputtering, unable to believe her ears.

There were giggles filling the classroom, and then a voice from behind her said, "Well, how about it? Will you marry me?"

Kody leaned behind her on the door frame, a bunch of flowers in one hand. "You did great, kids," he said with a wink to her class. "I think we caught her off guard."

"You certainly did," Susan said, shaking her head. "I was not expecting a proposal, and I'd have never expected a proposal like this."

But as she glanced around the room and saw the hopeful eyes on her students, she understood at once. Kody, the school, the kids—they were a package deal. He wanted to include them and make them feel a part of things. He always had.

"Well?" he asked with a grin as he brought one hand to his chest. "Are you going to break my heart in front of all these witnesses?"

Susan laughed, and then took the flowers from him, as she wrapped her arms around his neck. "I'd be happy to marry you," she told him.

As she stepped back, she added, "And stay teacher for you wonderful children."

Suddenly, she was crushed in a hug from all sides by her students, and more streamed into the classroom, along with their teachers.

"You planned this?" Susan laughed. "Everyone is here?"

"I did," he agreed. "It's a big deal. Now, back to your desks, rascals."

The children giggled, and scampered back to their seats or classrooms. One by one, the teachers left too, whispering congratulations or patting her shoulder as they departed.

"I'll see you later." Kody grinned. "But, before I go, there's something I want to tell you."

"What's that?" Susan asked.

"Remember I said the kids and I are a package deal?" When she nodded, he added, "What I never told you, was something was missing. Your yes made it complete."

He turned and left, but called over his shoulder, "I'm claiming our first kiss later!"

Susan's face flamed, but the beaming smiles from all of her students eased her embarrassment.

"Miss Louden?" Josh asked.

"Yes, dear?" she said.

"I'm awfully glad you're staying around," Josh told her.

Susan noticed all of the children nodded, and she looked lovingly at each through her watery eyes. "I wouldn't leave you for anything. We are a family and belong together. You'll have me around for a long time."

"You promise?" a little girl asked.

"Better than that," Susan said, with a wink. "I bet on it."

Epilogue

Three years later

Kody walked past the row of classrooms where behind the doors, forty-two children sat, learning. Elsewhere on the grounds, another twenty, the older students, learned skills like carpentry and horse care. In town, three were with the doctor, learning all he could share.

"You should be proud of yourself," Mrs. Washington said, coming up to him. "A father to so many."

"I'm fortunate," Kody said. "I'm grateful to have each of these children, and to do my part in raising them."

"I'm grateful your investments have been so good, and that you've also been able to find those willing to sponsor the school. The cost is significant," Mrs. Washington said.

"Worth every dime," Kody said, stopping in front of Susan's classroom.

Mrs. Washington smiled, and continued down the hallway to a large bell, which she rang. One by one, the classroom doors opened, and children filed out neatly to go to their lunch.

Kody stuck his head inside. "I thought I'd escort you to lunch today," he said with a grin.

"All the way down to the dining room?" Susan teased.

"Nothing's too good for my wife." Kody winked. "Especially if it means I don't have to walk far."

Susan laughed and took his arm.

"Need anything for the classroom?" he asked her.

"Not a thing. We are well provided for," Susan assured him.

"Just let me know," Kody said, leading her to the dining room.

There were so many children, a second long table had been squeezed in. It was tight at times, but no one would have it any other way. Kody helped Susan in her seat and sat next to her.

A simple lunch, soup, rolls, and applesauce, but it hit the spot. As did the chatter going around the table.

Kody let his eyes fall on each of the children, and felt his heart swell with pride. Each had arrived lost, and lonely, hurt, and some starving. But now, every single one flourished. It did him good to see it.

"Where's Josh?" Kody said suddenly, tensing as he looked at Susan.

"It's Tuesday. His day to run the stable," she told him reassuringly.

Kody let out a breath and nodded. "That's right. I forgot. Thought it was Wednesday. I'll just go check on him when I leave."

"Father hen," Susan teased.

Kody just laughed. "I have to be. They are all mine, but somehow, him especially."

Susan just smiled.

Kody resumed spooning his soup. Later that night, when they were in their small cottage on the school property, sitting before the crackling fire in the stone fireplace, he was going to tell her just how much he loved her, and how grateful he was that she was his too.

Right after Susan had said yes, Kody had rushed to tell his friend James, and his wife Grace, who had congratulated him. Both had been there at his wedding, as had their children.

Alice was a right lovely thing, both inside and out, and had been asking if she might be allowed to come and learn how to be a teacher there. Kody was willing to bet she'd be a fine one and, having been without a father for a time, likely to connect well with the children.

"Everything's working out well," he said quietly, nodding in satisfaction.

"Is that a bet you are thinking about?" Susan teased, "or a comment."

"Just thinking," Kody told her. "It all fell into place. The school, the children, you. I couldn't be happier with the way life has turned out for me."

He swallowed hard. It was true. Five-year-old Kody, hungry and hurting, could never have imagined a life where he had all he wanted, and so much he could provide for others. He was proud of that fact.

He was also amazed by the fact that he had someone who loved him for himself. That was also something he never thought he'd have.

"I feel just the same," Susan murmured. She smiled at him. "You've done good."

"We've done good, Sunshine," Kody told her. "I can't do this without you."

"You won't ever have to," Susan told him. "You, the school, the children, me? We're a package deal."

"I love you, Susan," Kody whispered.

"And I love you," she answered.

Note from Author

Thank you for taking the time to read Mail-Order Gambler!

Could I ask for one small favor? Reviews like yours on Amazon mean so much to me and help others to find my books! Even just a single line means a lot!

Also...

Want a FREE book?

Stop by my website to get your no strings attached **FREE book**. It's my gift to you, as a thank you for reading this one.

www.sarahlambbooks.com

Want more?

If you enjoyed this story, you might also like to read about how James the gunslinger, and Grace met, in *A Gunslinger for Grace*

She didn't expect a gunslinger to answer her ad. Now, things have gotten complicated.

Grace just can't do it alone anymore. When her husband died, he left her with a store to run and two children to take care of. Now, her son is friends with the wrong crowd and her daughter keeps sneaking out. When a string of vandalisms hit her store and the sheriff does nothing, she's more than desperate for help and puts an ad in the newspaper.

James is passing through town after dropping off a criminal at the local jail. A gunslinger by trade, he moves from town to town looking for high-paying work. When he chances upon Grace's ad, the thought of home cooked meals and an opportunity to rest for a while tempts him, and he applies.

No one else wants the job, so Grace reluctantly accepts his offer. But how will a gunslinger be able to help her with her children, the store, and stop the robberies? And why does she feel so drawn to the man who is like no one she's ever met?

https://www.amazon.com/Gunslinger-Grace-Sarah-Lamb-ebook/dp/B0C5FT56DN

***

You also might enjoy reading about Andrew and Evie, in *To Overcome Betrayal*.

At what point does a misunderstanding turn into a lie?

Evie Brown would do anything for her uncle, the only family she's ever known. So when he comes to her with a desperate plea to help save his home and business, she takes the only job she can find—housemaid for a rancher she knows nothing about. Making friends with a ranch hand who literally sweeps her off her feet is just a bonus.

Andrew Radcliffe is tired of every woman he's ever met only interested in his money. Giving up on love, he focuses on expanding his ranch, and demanding loyalty from those who work for him. Mistaken by Evie for a servant in his own home, he plays along. At first, he enjoys the chance to learn more about the spirited young woman working for him. But complications arise as he falls in love with her.

Just after Evie admits to Andrew she's fallen for him, her uncle arrives with a scheme. Now Evie faces an impossible choice—lose the man she's fallen in love with, or turn her back on her family. Who will she betray? And when Evie discovers Andrew isn't just a ranch hand, she's certain no matter her decision, a happy ending is heartbreakingly out of reach.

https://www.amazon.com/Overcome-Betrayal-Hearts-Wounded-Spirits-ebook/dp/B0CYYFK6CK

***

Can't get enough Mail-Order husbands? Look for Mail-Order Tailor releasing soon, and enjoy *Mail-Order Teacher* now!

He thought he was heading to a teaching job, not that of a husband. Now what?

Samuel Donner, an experienced schoolteacher with a steely gaze and a firm grip on his principles, arrives in the dusty town of Cottonwood Falls answering their call for help. He's determined to bring order to chaos and transform the unruly children into well-educated citizens. His first target: the blatant disregard for attendance.

Abigail Lees, a single mother of three, struggles to keep her head above water. When Samuel visits, warning that her eldest son, Thomas, needs to attend school more often, she's surprised. Unbeknownst to her, Thomas has taken on the responsibility of providing for the family, sacrificing his education in the process.

Torn between his duty to the town and his growing affection for Abigail, and the fact another woman insists he's her mail-order husband, Samuel finds himself in a difficult position. He wants to help Thomas and Abigail, but adhering to his promise to the school board, and fending off unwanted advances, proves increasingly challenging.

Then Thomas is accused of a serious crime, and Samuel must reach a decision. Will he stand by the boy, even if it means jeopardizing his reputation and potentially betraying the trust of the community? And can his love for Abigail survive the storm of doubt and suspicion that threatens to engulf them all?

https://www.amazon.com/Mail-Order-Teacher-Honorable-Sarah-Lamb-ebook/dp/B0CQ3WZCFN

About the Author

Sarah writes captivating characters and clean romance that's anything BUT boring! From heartbreaking moments to heartwarming tales, get swept away in either historical or small town romance that pulls you in until the last page.

Nestled in the Blue Ridge Mountains of Virginia where she's married to her Texan husband, you'll find Sarah creating her next book, homeschooling her two boys, or volunteering in her community.

Want more of Sarah's books? Find them all on Amazon!

https://www.amazon.com/stores/Sarah-Lamb/author/B098H3SGLK

There are other great books in this series as well!

Find all the Mail-Order Husband books on Amazon!

https://www.amazon.com/dp/B0CKV92Y7D
Want more of Sarah's books? Find them all on Amazon!
https://www.amazon.com/stores/Sarah-Lamb/author/B098H3SGLK

www.ingramcontent.com/pod-product-compliance
Lightning Source LLC
Chambersburg PA
CBHW022020170626
46808CB00003B/1003